Purgatory

They came in the night and took away every inhabitant of the isolated mining town they could capture. Men, women and the one child were taken from the town that they rightly called Purgatory. But one man who had fought heroically against the invaders, John King, whom they had left for dead, was left to fight back against the biggest injustice of his life. With little left to lose, he was going to track down the men who had taken what was his, and get his revenge for his people.

This was no common raid on a small town. Helped in his quest by some unexpected allies, King soon discovers that his task is more difficult than even he realized. Who is the mysterious Valsquez, and what makes him more than a common bandit? King finds out only too soon when he has gone over the brink and into the madness of a revolution in the making.

Purgatory

Alex Hawksville

A Black Horse Western

ROBERT HALE

© Alex Hawksville 2018
First published in Great Britain 2018

ISBN 978-0-7198-2788-4

The Crowood Press
The Stable Block
Crowood Lane
Ramsbury
Marlborough
Wiltshire SN8 2HR

www.bhwesterns.com

Robert Hale is an imprint
of The Crowood Press

Typeset by
Derek Doyle & Associates, Shaw Heath
Printed and bound in Great Britain by
4Bind Ltd, Stevenage, SG1 2XT

CHAPTER ONE

Dirt, grime, the taste of defeat, face in the earth, barely breathing, choked up and ready to die in this year of our Lord 1895. He heaved himself convulsively upwards, loose, black debris falling from his shoulders, then promptly fell on to his back. Lying there for what seemed like an eternity, every bone in his body aching, he gathered together what was left of him.

'Maria' – at last a word escaped from his cracked lips. 'Maria, Ranald, Ben' – then he heaved himself to his feet again, swaying where he stood, and surveyed the ruin of what had been his home. Scrabbling forwards he pulled up wooden supports, bits of roof and wall, saying their names over and over again, desperate to find his wife and the boys.

The first person he found was his wife. The explosion had pushed the old-fashioned cast-iron stove into her body, driving it into the boards of the floor. She was dead all right, as dead as the lump of iron that had killed her, an indentation on the side of her head. Not far away he heaved up another section of the wall, and found little Ranald lying there, a bloody mess where a spar of wood from the wall's supporting frame had splintered off, tearing through his vulnerable young body.

There was no sign of his older son, though he searched on through the ruins of what had once been their home, with all that was left of his ebbing strength. There was one faint ray of hope, then, that young Ben had got away.

Then he was overcome by a black wave of darkness and fatigue that he could no longer resist. He fell to the ground and lay there under the midday sun, knowing nothing about the passing of time. While he lay there for what seemed like another eternity his senses were blurred – then consciousness returned, and he got to his feet and staggered over to the water butt that was used when it was raining. He took a long drink of the liquid and splashed water into his eyes.

He could not shake off the idea that none of this was happening, that he was having a dream – no, not a dream, a nightmare, one of those when you care so much for your family that you dream of someone hurting them and you think it has happened, but it's not true, it's the stuff of hell.

Except this was one case where the nightmare had come true.

He looked around the town that had been built on the last gold rush to be seen in the West. It was a valley across from where the Mexican territories had once been, in the south of what was now the state of Texas – and a hotly disputed borderland between the two countries. This was a valley known as El Gordo. In the old days it had just been a place on the cattle drive between Mexico and Dodge City.

John King knew all these things, and he cursed the day he had come to El Gordo with his family in search of a better life – a life that had ended right here and now.

He sat by the ruins of his house, head sunk on his chest, as one by one those who had been out prospecting when the attack happened, drifted back into what had been the village. He heard shouts of anger and pure rage, saw men getting weapons ready, but still did nothing.

Jos Carter, an old friend of the family, was the first to approach him. Carter reached out a firm hand and pulled him to his feet.

'Hell, we knew they was in the area, but we never thought this would happen!'

Neither of them needed to say anything else: they both knew they were talking about the bandits who had come to the town known as Purgatory. At one time the name had seemed like a joke. They also both knew that at least one of them had far more pressing concerns.

'A direct hit,' said Carter, 'and I guess you had the worst luck of all – your home was the biggest target, and they just plain bombed you.'

'They had a tube of some kind that they held, and which shot a bomb,' said his companion

7

shakily. 'They got us first time, got us all.'

He stopped talking for a moment as the picture of what had happened passed through his head: young Ben picking up a rifle and running for the door, screaming that he was going to stop the bad men – his father turning to him, yelling him to remain where he was, his last memory before the blackness that engulfed him.

'Where's the wife and the young 'un?' asked Carter, but the way King turned his head away as he was asked the question told him all he needed to know.

'The others – they've got no reason to stay here – the gold is running out anyway – and most of 'em have no one to worry about.' He didn't add that of all the people there, King had been the one with the most to lose, but the words hung in the air anyway.

'Then you'd better get going,' said King. 'No use hanging around for more of the same.'

'Trouble came here and left,' said Carter, 'and the wisest thing for me to do would be to run like hell, but I'm staying here to help you. Heck, I wouldn't be here in the first place if you hadn't patched me up after that shoot-out over a claim.'

Carter stopped talking then. He was there for a man who had just lost everything. He led John over to something that was barely recognizable as a shack – it was about the height of a man and seemed to be partly constructed of canvas, partly from wood, with one wall made of adobe, and a roof that was just a simple piece of corrugated iron flecked with rust.

He led his friend in through the low doorway and rescued a bottle from a hidden corner, and poured some of the rotgut into two battered old mugs. Neither of them said anything, but just drank the contents of their respective containers.

King slumped down again, and sat that way for several long minutes, then raised his head and looked directly at his companion.

'I need a spade, and transport.'

'You ain't in any condition to do anything. Bed down for a while. We'll do what has to be done on the morrow, first thing, and then we'll get you out of here.' But this wasn't what his friend wanted, and King got to his feet and went outside, staggering as he did so. The attack had happened in the mid-afternoon, but now it was getting towards twilight. Carter gave a sigh and followed him out. The place had plenty of shovels, it being a mining community, albeit one that was rapidly emptying of people even before the attack.

Carter fetched the tools and equipment his companion needed. Luckily most of the horses had been corralled in a fold of the valley, so it was easy to fetch these.

King worked methodically, a man with a mission. He put his wife on one of her favourite cloths, a cotton wrap covered in flower patterns, one of her few luxuries. He kissed her on the forehead before sealing her into the cloth with gut line, sewing it up with expert strokes.

That was bad enough, but he almost broke down when he had to wrap his dead son in a grey blanket. The boy's face was intact, and it was the last thing his father saw before his son, too, was sealed away for good.

Carter helped his friend put the bodies over the backs of their horses, and they made their way to the graveyard at the other end of town in a silence only broken by the sound of clopping hoofs – what was there to say?

On the way there they were joined by two men almost as big as Carter. One was dark-haired and dark-eyed, in contrast to Carter who had the fair skin of his British ancestors. He wore a gun belt with a weapon on his right-hand side, and there was a look about him that said he had seen a lot of death in his time, some of it by his own hand.

The other man was as tall as Carter, but of slighter build. He was not as swarthy as the other, and he wore the kind of dusty clothes that proclaimed him to be a miner – this time one who had come back to the town only to hear the devastating news of what had happened to King and the townspeople.

There was a wooden fence about the height of a man's waist that separated the graveyard from the rest of town. Most of the tombstones, where they existed, were roughly carved out of the local stone. That was one thing about this area: there was no shortage of materials.

In the gathering twilight the four men fell to

work, and it wasn't long before the graves were dug. The two bodies were placed in the ground swathed in their makeshift shrouds. Before the earth was shovelled back on to his wife and child, King stood still and gave a eulogy to his loved ones.

'I came here to make my money and care for you all. My youngest, you were born and died here. My wife, my Maria, you would not stay behind: you insisted on coming here, you said it would be an adventure, and I gave in because I was selfish and I wanted your company. We have all paid for my selfishness.' Then he offered up a brief prayer, said grimly, to show that he could barely believe in a God who would let his loved ones be taken like this.

Once the earth was piled back on the new graves he stood back, shovel in hand, looking like a statue of a man in the semi-darkness; then he turned and walked out of the graveyard, and fell to the ground as if he had been struck with a club.

CHAPTER TWO

King lay like one dead for so long that Carter thought his friend had passed away during the night. But at last he awoke, saw to his toilet without a word, and returned to the shack belonging to his friend.

'I'm hungry,' he said. Luckily Carter had sufficient food for both – corn, beans, some bread and some beef preserved in salt. Tinned foods had come in too, and he had some tinned pork and even some sweet strawberry preserve for putting on locally baked wheat biscuits.

They ate the food cold for fear that a fire would make them a target. Although it was dawn, it was the very start of the day so they were still shadows to each other. But as King sat and ate his food, he could see that Carter's den was almost empty.

'What's going on?' he asked.

'We're getting out,' said Carter, 'the rest of us, I mean. You're coming with us.'

As the light arose the two men who had helped

see King's family to their final resting place the previous night, Will Vetters and Ant Sutton, arrived,
dressed for the journey, wearing greatcoats that
they would not discard until later when the sun
arose.

'Well,' said Will, the big, dark-haired man, 'time
for us to get out of here.'

'He's right,' said Ant. 'We don't know when
they'll come back to get more of what they can take
from us – food, money, goods. We can't assume
they're done with the town.' Jos Carter didn't say
anything, but it was plain that he agreed with his
two companions. There was nothing left for them
now in this terrible place that had taken so much
from them all.

King stood up. There was a scar on his forehead
that still glistened raw in the faint morning sun.

'You guys did me a favour last night. I would
never have managed without you, but I can't go.'
His three companions stared at him.

'You really don't seem to understand do you? I
have two sons, they've got my eldest boy. They've
got Ben.'

'Then I guess it's best that we lay out what's happened here,' said Carter, with a look on his face that
indicated he didn't want the matter to be put in this
way. 'They've got your boy, yes, but do you think
he'll survive for long? Hell, I don't even like saying
this after what's happened here, but we have to face
up to reality.'

'Reality? I'll tell you what reality is. We were

13

raided by Valsquez, that's the reality of the situation. All these years we've known about the unrest – hell, we were even raided by them other bandits a hundred times.'

'They was thieves in the night,' said Sutton, 'when the thievery happened we could deal with it, horses, hardware, food. But there was plenty of us in those days, and more often than not we caught the culprits and strung 'em up.'

'Valsquez is different,' said King. 'Anyone who's been back to Houston or any big town knows that he's been in the papers, the *Southern Star* and *The Sun*. They've pasted plenty of items about what he's doing. Hell, he even had the attention of the state governor.'

'We all saw what he was up to,' said Will Vetters, breaking his silence, but looking directly at the man who had been his friend and a leading light, a leader of their community. 'It was, I guess, a case of divide and conquer. He felt that these here lands belonged to his people and he was putting up real legal challenges to get the land back. He had money, plenty of it, too, which they said he had got by carrying out raids on the very land he was claiming.'

'Couldn't have improved his temper when he brought his cases and they was all knocked back by the courts,' said Sutton. 'But how do we know that this here raid came from Valsquez?'

'I know,' said King, his expression turning to stone.

'But how?' persisted Sutton.

'Because he was the man who fired that bomb at my home,' said King. 'I've seen his picture in the papers, he's a big man, almost as big as you Carter, with a way of staring straight forward and eyes as blue as the sea. His face was blacked up like a lot of them, but it was him all right.'

'But you didn't see his face properly,' Carter persisted, 'and how do you know he has that kind of eyes?'

'Because I've read descriptions of him,' said King. 'And he had that air of power; you just recognize it when you see it.'

'We ain't got time to keep up this discussion,' warned Sutton. 'I'll ask you one more time, are you coming with us?'

'No,' said John King, but so quietly it was almost a whisper, 'I guess I have to go where my stars take me. I don't blame the three of you. There's a trading post back east a little ways. I have plenty of money. I'll go there and weapon up, because if I'm going to get my boy back I'll need to give the both of us the best chance we can have. What about you three?'

'We'll ride back to the city. We have gold,' said Vetters. 'Ain't that about right, you guys?' The other two looked uncomfortable, but they mumbled replies in the affirmative.

'Look at it this way,' said Carter, 'they came here on a raid, a whole mess of them, they took most of the townspeople and killed others, and they left you for dead. They're organized, and they have more weapons than you can shake a stick at. I hate to say this, John, but Ben's as good as dead. Hell, you've been struck so hard. . . .' he broke off.

'I understand that,' said King, 'but those miners and their girls, I was kind of an unofficial mayor of this hell-hole, the only one they could rely on. I don't know why the heck Valsquez and his bastards have taken them, but I sure as hell know that I'll go down fighting to defend what is mine.'

There was no more time. Nobody wanted to be in the place rightly called Purgatory when there was a possibility of more raiders coming back and taking what they wanted. John Fortune turned and watched as his three friends rode back towards a civilization that had been so badly missing from where they had lived and worked during the best years of their lives.

He had no doubt they had enough money to start their own businesses once they got back to the city. They rode off with one final look back to see if he was going to change his mind, but he sat on his grey in the gathering sunlight like a statue, immovable as he watched them go.

He had a spare pack-horse with him, and he rode with the two animals away from the tributary of the Brazos that had been the main lifeblood of the town they had called Purgatory, and the rocky landscape of El Gordo valley – a valley so lacking in resources that most of the goods, including the building materials, had to be brought into the area. He was heading for the trading post run by a Kiowa called Red Bear, who had long provided goods for the miners coming out to this area. King had enough money with him, and a Colt on each hip, but he was not stupid enough to think that just one man with two guns was enough to take on a small army.

How many men did Valsquez have? That was the question. He wasn't just going to go in with guns blazing, and Red Bear might help him recruit a few helpers. Then he heard a thundering of hoofs on the trail behind him: he was going to face an enemy sooner than he had thought.

CHAPTER THREE

King was mounted on a grey mare called Meg. The raiders had made off with most of the best horses, but the grey had grit, and her ears flattened back as he gave her an urgent command to gallop. She picked up speed over the rough land, and soon the sound of the pursuing hoofs began to fade away as she ate up the scrubland. Even his pack horse was finding it hard to keep up.

He might be running from a bullet in the back, but if they wanted to pursue him in this way it was going to cost them dear. Still going at that break-neck speed he crouched low in the saddle, his face against Meg's mane.

'Hello,' cried out a familiar voice. For a moment he thought it was some kind of trick, and that the enemy was using someone familiar to trap him, but the desperation in that one cry made him slow Meg down, and he twisted his body in the big cowboy saddle to look behind him. There was Carter, and behind him two other mounted figures at a greater distance so he couldn't make out their faces – but just the same he knew who they were. He slowed the mare down to almost a complete halt, but gradually so she didn't damage her ligaments, appreciating that a sudden halt could make her lame. He liked Meg, but that wasn't the only reason: a lame horse was useless as far as his task was concerned.

His task was the important thing: he was full of grief and pain over the death of his wife and son, though living in Purgatory, where death had been a daily occurrence for many, had taught him to hold his emotions tight to his chest. This was a world of life and death, that was plain – but when that death was to the ones who would have made your future bright, this created a fire in your brain that would not go out. Then Vetters, Sutton and Carter were beside him.

'You blamed idiot!' said Carter. 'Nearly broke ma neck there when ma durned horse stumbled!'

'Serves you right for trying to sneak up on a man,' said King, trying to disguise the relief in his voice. 'You never were the best rider Carter, but I can't say I'm not glad to see you. You too, Will and Ant – never thought I'd see any of you again.'

'Well, we got to talking,' said Carter. 'None of us has got any family 'cept our brothers and sisters, and we're younger than you, and we'll have some kind of life when we go back to town.'

'But this here Valsquez,' said Ant, 'well, he's done something that dishonours Texas and takes away

19

from our homeland, on top of being a murdering bastard.'

'So we decided to go along with you just to see what the lie of the land was,' said Will, 'couldn't stand the thought of you getting in there by yourself and having all the fun.'

King nodded, unable to speak for a moment.

'OK,' he said finally, keeping his voice as casual as he could, 'let's get to this trading post.'

Red Bear seemed able to pick up information from thin air, because when they arrived at the trading post he evidently already knew about the raid on Purgatory. He was a small but square-set man who wore traditional buckskin garments and a head-band, and had his long black hair plaited so that it hung down his back. His recent forefathers had seen the way the wind was blowing and had decided that to keep some of their way of life they would fall in with the white man. By being traders they at least proved useful to the white man's way of life, and it meant they could still live on the land and keep some of their traditional ways.

The trading post was a big building, but less than fancy, with walls made from a mixture of brick and adobe, and a roof of red tiling. It was a sign of the times – they were in the late nineties by now – that Indians were able to employ white workers and sell guns to travellers.

'Bad thing,' said Red Cloud as they walked around the trading post picking up the dry goods that they would need for their trip. 'Bad news for this whole area. This Mexican, he is making it sore for everyone.'

'What do you know?' asked King, burning for information, 'and how?'

'How you think we get supplies? Get them from all over, from across the borders too, preserves and other foods,' said Red Cloud, who was fairly elderly and did not pull his punches.

'It's been less than a day,' said King. 'Now what do you know?'

'Only that they follow the cattle trail down beside the Brazos,' said Red Cloud, 'that they take them to some place of their choice, that they armed. Say,' he looked more closely at his visitor, 'you John King, did good business in past, how come not captured?'

'I don't want to talk about it,' said King, turning away.

'Bad things happen,' said Red Bear. This made King turn back to him again, just as he was turning away to pick up more supplies.

'Bad men, in power of the leader, they roam across land and attack people on small holdings, little farms, people like you.'

'I've never heard much about this,' said King grimly. But then he paused, reflecting that in El Gordo Valley they had been very much isolated in a part of the land where news rarely filtered through from the outside world.

'Been much bad lately,' said the old man, 'they stir because they say this land belong to Mexico, not Texas.'

'You mean the US,' said Carter, who had been listening nearby. The old man shrugged.

'It all the same to my people. All land the same, part of the world, we went where we like, only your kind divide up the land and use it to hurt each other.'

King was not about to allow himself to be given a lecture by an old man, and turned away to continue his task of finding the supplies he wanted; but he soon came back demanding a selection of guns, rifles and bullets that made the seasoned trader raise his bushy eyebrows. The weapons were not on open display, but were kept in a sealed area that had to be unlocked by the old Indian. King also discovered a small keg of gunpowder in the arms store, which he also picked up.

'This cost much money,' said Red Bear.

'I'm good for it,' said King, and he was.

He questioned the old Indian for a little while longer, but in the way of these things the old man had heard more rumours than he had information. The route to the trading post had taken them well away from the Brazos, and King did not want to waste any more time discussing the possibilities with the trader. It might well have been worth waiting to get more information from the customers who arrived from time to time during the day, but time was a luxury they did not have.

However, King was not one to discuss his plans in front of those who would freely gossip about what they had heard, and he also knew that Red Bear did not discriminate between those who came to see him. He would just as readily trade with the Mexicans, although he would be wary about selling them weapons, since the state of Texas frowned upon that kind of sale, seeing it as a potentially traitorous act.

Even so, King knew that his very presence here was alarming enough to alert any dictator who got wind of what he was doing. The way news spread he knew that word would get out soon enough, but if they could keep any discussions just between themselves, they might be able to get a few days grace before anyone knew what they were up to.

They rode back towards the Brazos; it had taken them several hours to get to the trading post, and the noonday sun was high in the sky and it was hot. They stopped in an arroyo and made sure that the horses were watered by digging down and getting to the life-giving liquid that trickled below, normally hidden from sight. The horses were an essential part of their plans, and if they were injured in any way they would never make any headway against the men who had decimated Purgatory.

'What are we going to do now?' asked Carter as they rested and ate some beef jerky and beans.

'There's a smallholding to the south of here,' said King, 'it belongs to a farmer and his daughter, and it's just a few miles from the Brazos. A man called Hawkes. Looks like a hawk too, sharp-eyed and cunning and able to look after his kin.'

'How do you know about him?' asked Sutton.

23

'Funnily enough, we met at the trading post,' said King. 'Turned out he was one of the old cattle traders, and when that business died the death he just plain stayed on.'

They all knew what he was talking about, because although none of them had been trail riders, they all knew about the great hordes of cattle that once passed through this area, hundreds of thousands every year.

'It's amazing,' said Vetters 'that a business could die away so quickly.'

'There was sound economic reasons for that,' replied King. 'The railways spread over the whole country, and then they brought in those new-fangled refrigeration carriages.'

'Well, that makes a lot more sense,' said Sutter. 'Instead of beeves being on their feet for days, weeks, even months, they're just bred where they are and transported by railway. Makes a heck of a lot more sense.'

'But what you don't seem to understand is that the death of the cattle trails is the very reason why the present unrest is happening,' said King.

'Too right, I don't rightly understand,' said Carter. 'You wouldn't think a few missing beeves would be the cause of unrest amongst the Mexes.' This was a nickname for the troublesome border raiders.

'Simple enough,' said King. 'Thousands of cattle, hundreds of thousands really, translates into not just hundreds of thousands of dollars, but millions, and if your business depends on protecting your cattle, you protect them.'

They had to admit that this was true, that the trail riders had not just been there to herd the cattle along the Brazos, they had also been there to protect the animals that would provide them with a pay and a bonus if they got them safely to the rail-heads at Kansas. Any raiders would have been met with short shrift from guns and rifles, not to mention the risk of being crushed to death by countless hoofs.

'There's another factor too,' said Vetters. 'The Brazos was real important during the Civil War, especially to the rebels. The North built forts all over the place, and army units were stationed all over the place right up until the late eighties.'

'Yep, and that meant that bandits of any kind would be picked up on and quelled before they was able to do much damage to any kind of business in this area,' said King.

There was a look on his face that meant he was suddenly deep in thought.

'What's wrong?' asked Carter. He was no expert in the human mind, but he reckoned that if a man had taken the kind of loss borne by King it might be enough to unhinge him through grief and rage. The calmness shown by John King seemed to him nothing more than a miracle, but it was a miracle that could end at any time, and perhaps this was the first sign.

'Nothing,' said King, 'just got a sudden notion,

and that's all it is right now.' He got up from the ledge of stone he had been sitting on at the edge of the dry riverbed. 'Time for us to have a little practice, guys.'

'Don't rightly know what you mean,' said Carter.

'We just about bought out that Injun,' replied his friend. 'Put it like this. You're all miners, and I'm a man of peace, or I was. One thing is, we're all in shape due to our lifestyles, so we won't fatigue too easy. But we got to see that we can shoot straight.'

'We've all been armed for the whole time in Purga,' said Vetters, 'me and Sutton here, we had our fair share of fights, good and bad, we've been wounded too, all three of us, and I can assure you, friend, we can mount a real good defence if we need to.'

'It's not defence I'm thinking of,' said King, 'and when it comes to mounting that attack we'll have to be right in there.'

Reluctantly the other three agreed, although Carter had the feeling that target practice was being carried out as much for King's sake as for that of his companions. They set up various targets – sometimes bits of rock, or bits of branch roughly about the size of a man which they found at the bottom of the arroyo, swept down there by the winter floods – and practised their aim, both at close range and from a distance. And they all discovered – much to the chagrin of Sutton and Vetters, who had been so bold in their prediction of their shared ability – that they were not quite as good at gunplay as they had imagined.

It wasn't just a matter of learning how to shoot effectively and fast, it also taught them that hand guns and rifles could jam, and that they had to be ready with another on hand. It also taught them the value of keeping their steeds nearby so they could jump into the saddle and ride off at a moment's notice.

They were preparing for war.

CHAPTER FOUR

They all steadily improved, and by the late after-noon, and after making an inventory of their goods, King deemed them good enough to move on.

'We had to practise our moves in a remote loca-tion like this,' he told them. 'Any closer to where we're going and shots could alarm the locals, not all of whom are friendly towards us.'

'I hope this Hawkes feller is hospitable enough,' said Carter. 'We all need a drink.'

'We won't be drinking,' said King reasonably enough. 'What we're depending on is keeping clear heads and using the element of surprise.'

'What can four of us do?' asked Vetters suddenly, with a lack of confidence that would have surprised anyone who knew the man from before.

'We can do a lot more than you think,' replied King, 'besides, we're not going into this alone.'

'There's something you haven't told us?' asked Sutton.

'Hawkes has a lot of animals to look after, so he

28

has farmhands who'll join us in the fight, perhaps double our numbers.'

'I'm beginning to see why you brought so many weapons,' said Carter.

They rode on through the scrubland and into a landscape that undulated before them so they had to top a rise before coming into sight of the Hawkes' spread. The ranch was still some distance away when King held up a commanding hand, with the others halting behind him.

'Whoah,' he said, 'there's something wrong.' A line of black smoke quite unlike that of a normal fire curled up through the trees.

'Get your weapons ready,' said King grimly as he spurred his horse onwards without waiting for the rest.

Valsquez rode at the head of the column. Most of the people behind him, over a hundred of them, were on foot, while his men were mounted on horseback. They were following the old cattle trail down beside the Brazos. It was by no means a clear run, because even in the few years since the great movements of cattle had ceased, some parts of the trail had become overgrown. This did not bother him in the least because if the undergrowth hindered his movements it would also stop anyone from pursuing him and his men effectively.

Like John King, there was an air of solid purpose about Jorge Valsquez. He was a slimmer man than King, and had the dark skin that his ancestors had acquired from spending so much time in the sun. His hands were long too, and he had wide shoulders. When he took off his hat and swept a hand through his thick dark hair, it was evident that he was young too, younger than his military bearing and his air of command seemed to indicate. He was barely out of his twenties. His face was not conventionally handsome but he had big dark eyes and a wide, expressive mouth. Like many of his people, his teeth were not well cared for, but like most he had a fierce look that indicated he was not about to put up with anything that might be imposed upon him.

He wore a blue, military-style coat, and his hat, instead of being some shapeless covering, was like the hat of an admiral, being tri-cornered and lined with gold braid, as was his tunic.

It was not the way he had been dressed on the raid with his men in El Gordo: during the raid he had dressed like a man of action in a black uniform, face blacked, as he fought against and captured the gringos. As soon as the campaign was successfully completed he had felt obliged to dress like a leader again. One of the penalties of leading a people, those who liked to see the symbolic before them, was in the shape of how leader behaved and dressed.

There was a slight stir as another man rode forwards on a big black Mexican horse. These horses had been bred bigger deliberately, also as a symbol of power. He made no quarter for those who might be in his path and there were cries of fear as the respective walkers flung themselves out of his way. Those who did move were forced back into place by another rider coming up from behind who lashed out with a many tailed whip known as a Cat. It was an effective way of cowing a man as it lashed at him multiple times.

'What do you have to tell me, Hernandez?' asked Valquez as the other man gave him a smart salute.

'Not much, so that is the good news,' said Victor Hernandez. He was a tall man, not as slight as his leader, being a good few years older and much stockier. Most of those who were involved in this insurrection were young – the young always wanted revolution, but he was an elder statesman and guide to them. 'We lost a few of them to the cold during the night, but that is the kind of thing that can be expected.'

'Regrettable,' said Valsquez, 'the more of them we have, the better will be the results when we arrive.'

The fact was that due to the nature of the campaign the previous evening it had been impossible to provide enough food and shelter for their captives along the way.

'General, I hardly believed this would happen, until it did,' said Hernandez.

'You were a big part of our success, Victor,' said Valsquez. 'You fought with a ferocity that I could not believe. You went into their dwellings and captured us many of those we might have missed, forcing them into the streets and herding them like cattle. Most of all, it was you who directed me to bomb the most dangerous place, which I bombed, preventing more of our men from falling.'

'I did what I had to do.'

'When you have some thirty men,' said Valsquez, 'every man who dies dilutes your chances of success. We have several injuries, but we didn't lose too many of our compatriots thanks to you, my second-in-command.'

'I was only doing my duty,' said Hernandez. His face grew darker as, inside his mind he went back to his past. 'Doing my duty not just to you, my General, but to my family.'

'Yes, you have told me some of this before,' said Valsquez hastily. He had enough on his mind concerning the recent past without digging into distant injustices; But Hernandez was on his high horse both literally and figuratively.

'The Westerners, as they called themselves, came here and took the land off my ancestors. We owned El Gordo, we named it, it was ours, not theirs. And the governments, they were traitors to us, they settled there, selling off what was ours for a few million dollars worth of gold. That valley has paid back the gringo many more times that over the years. We were robbed, my family reduced to having to work selling goods and services like any shopkeeper just to survive and continue our line. As far as I am concerned that valley is still *mine*.'

'Never mind, my friend, we are nearly there,' said

Valquez, 'then we will set to work and rebuild and make our stand, we will stir the people into revolution and we will take back more than an isolated valley.'

'Very well,' said Hernandez. He rode forward, eager to get to the end of the journey, his eyes blazing with a light that showed him to be a true fanatic for the cause.

Behind the two leaders struggled the people who had once been the inhabitants of Purgatory. They were kept in line both by riders and by armed soldiers on foot. Most of the enforced evacuees were male, but there were at least twenty women amongst them, and one small boy. At the time of the raid there had been one proper family left in town. The mining of gold and silver that had powered the settlement had declined drastically in the two years before the raid, which meant that only die-hard souls remained in a town so isolated that some people had never even heard of the place.

The young boy stumbled onwards with a look of sullen anger in his eyes. The townspeople had walked for many miles the previous night, and then when it was too dark to continue, they had been herded together like cattle and made to lie down in a clearing, guarded by men with whips and guns.

They had no shelter at all, and had to huddle together just for basic warmth. The young boy was lucky, because some of the women had protected him, and when he got up, although cold, he had not suffered too much due to the elements. But two

of the men and one of the women were not so lucky,
and once the others had done the basics and were
herded back together, the bodies had been picked
up and thrown into the river by the captives, at the
urging of their captors. It was evident that the revo-
lutionaries wanted to leave as little trace of their
passing as possible.

There was no food, but the young boy had found
some wild apples and passed them around, and they
drank freely from the waters of the Brazos. But they
were not given much time to do this before they
were whipped into shape and made to continue the
long trek. The young boy, called Ben, had one
thought in his head: somehow, sometime, he was
going to kill Valsquez.

CHAPTER FIVE

Sitting on his mare below the ranch, with the trees still intervening, King stared at the greasy column of black smoke for a short while.

'Dismount and back me up,' he said, clutching a Winchester in his hand. This was an '88 model, more modern with better lines and better action, but still recognizable as the offspring of the '73, the rifle that had won the war as far as colonizing the US went.

He ran through the trees towards the ranch that belonged to his old friend. There he saw a sight that dismayed his heart. The main building was not merely on fire – it was too late for that, the fire had already taken place, and the building was a burnt-out shell. The two men there were both dressed in the dark peasant clothes of the Mexican peon. This was a small matter because the sight of such men this close to the border was a common sight, but since the partition of lands had taken place between Texas and its neighbour they were not seen as often near the smaller ranches – and certainly not within the vicinity of a once burning building. There was a viscous, oily stink in the air that choked the back of his throat, and the air was full of fine, black floating particles that he felt drift across his face like falling snowflakes as he ran.

The two men had lined, anxious faces, at least on what could be seen of their faces above the 'kerchiefs that covered their mouths and noses, and it was obvious that they had been making sure that the fire had done its job. But like all ranches, a number of outbuildings existed for use as storage units, and there was a stable capable of holding at least ten horses a short distance away from the ruined ranch house.

One of the peons had lighted a torch from the burning embers of the fire and he advanced towards the stable in a purposeful manner that meant he and his companion were going to finish the job they had started. They were oblivious, for the moment, to the new arrivals, and as they advanced King saw something that touched a raw nerve in him.

A young woman appeared briefly in front of one of the peons, coming out of the stable, holding out her hands. Only one of them seemed to be armed and he took a pot shot at her before she retreated to what shelter she had, the shot tearing wooden splinters off the stall where she had been standing.

'Hold up!' roared King, thudding his way towards the two men. The one with the gun turned and loosed off a shot at him – though luckily for King, the shot, hastily aimed, roared harmlessly past his head. And also luckily for Carter, who was close behind, the bullet whining between the two of them.

The trouble was, King had hesitated. It was not his job to take life, rather the opposite in fact. He had been the one medical expert in the town of Purgatory, falling into that role during the boom years when the population had risen to bursting, his services paid for in gold. He had never killed a man before, either in cold blood or in anger.

Like most other humans when pushed, pure instinct took over and his shot took the man full in the chest. His attacker gave one loud gasp and keeled forwards to the dark earth, where the bright red of his blood leaked from his body and mingled with the soil below him.

The second man made a tactical mistake: he yelled out in Spanish and snatched up his friend's weapon and aimed it at the two men, obviously ready to fire. Two gunshots later and he, too, was on the ground, the shots this time fired by Carter who was not about to risk his own person.

Carter ran forwards and exclaimed over the dying man:

'You fool,' he said, 'if you had just surrendered!'
The peon lifted his head and looked at Carter with bewildered eyes.

'We had to stop it,' he said. Then he babbled something in his own tongue and died.

'Hell, I don't know what's going on,' said Carter. 'These two were intent on destruction, and they wanted to kill that girl, too.'

Sutton and Vetters had arrived by then. Neither of them seemed to entirely know what to do, but King took the lead as usual.

'Wait here,' he told them, and advanced to the stable, where the horses, frightened by the smoke and the violence, were kicking in their stalls. He opened the one stall where there wasn't any noise, and was flung aside by an advancing demon. It was lucky that he had quick reactions because he managed to duck and pull back as an iron bar swished through the air, aimed at his head.

'What the hell?' he asked rhetorically. He pulled away as the girl moved back, dropped the length of metal and burst into tears. He respected what she had done: she couldn't know that they were acting as her rescuers – as far as she was concerned they might have been in league with her attackers.

'Look, Miss, I remember your father talking about you when we were having a drink or two together. You're Alice, aren't you?'

'Yes.' The girl was looking at him with wide eyes now; she was auburn-haired and very pretty – and fairly scared, too.

'I'll help you. Now where's your father?'

'He was in our home,' said the girl in a trembling voice. 'He's dead.'

'Hell,' said King grimly. 'Well, at least we got the bastards who did for him.'

38

'No, no, you don't understand, *they* didn't kill Father, *I* did.'

They made some sort of encampment in the old barn. The men had at least been systematic in the process of burning down the ranch and its surroundings. The girl kept well away from the men who were with her in the building, deliberately sitting at some distance from them.

'It's all right,' said King, 'we won't hurt you.'

'No,' she said, 'but I might harm *you*.'

King had little time for mysteries, but he felt that here was one he would like to solve before they went on their way, not least because he had liked Old Man Hawkes and wasn't satisfied with the little he knew. Besides, he and his men had to have somewhere to rest for the night, and despite what had happened to the ranch, the barn was a perfectly reasonable shelter for the four of them.

'What happened?' he asked wearily. The girl looked shrewdly from man to man.

'You all look weary,' she said, 'as if you've hardly slept – and you all have pack animals with you, so something's going on.' She bowed her head again, then felt the weight of their expectant silence. 'It all started with the woman and the baby.'

'What woman and what baby?' asked King.

'As you know, this entire area was once Mexican, and there are still many settlers living here with that type of ancestry. They have a particular fear of diseases, and the poor woman had been cast out by her local community. My father' – here her lips trembled, but she managed to continue – 'my father was the kindest of men, and he sheltered her. Then the baby died, and the woman too.'

'But what was the sickness?' asked King. The girl did not answer him for a long time.

'Then a couple of our riders became ill with the same thing. We sent for a doctor and he diagnosed that there was cholera on the farm – and I was the one who had been dealing with the sick woman. Then my father grew ill, and everyone fled. Those men, Miguel and Garonne, they were land workers for my father. Only two days ago they learned that my father had died. I was with him until the end.'

There was a general stir in the barn. Cholera was a highly contagious illness, and feared because once it was in a community it could spread and kill the old and the weak with frightening ease.

'The main thing was that I was the cause of the illness spreading to everyone I came into contact with,' said the girl. 'Seriously, I would leave right now and hope that you never regret the day you came into contact with Alice Hawkes.'

'You might have been in contact,' said Jos Carter with a forcefulness that partly concealed his good nature, 'but there's nothing to say that you caused anything – the original carrier could have spread the illness a long ways before you got involved.'

'I reckon we should stay,' said Sutton, drawing nods of agreement from the rest of the men. The girl looked at them with astonishment and fear.

40

'Why would you do that? It would be better for me if I were to disappear off the earth altogether.'

'I don't think so,' said King. 'Let me tell you a little tale. You see, we come from a mining community back there in El Gordo, on a tributary of the Brazos. Well, that town was full to bursting some five or six years ago. The gold and silver yields were high, and the place was packed – hell, we had our own saloons and gaming houses where gold dust was exchanged in gambling as soon as it was dug or panned.'

'What has this to do with me?' asked the girl.

'Well, the conditions weren't always what you call sanitary. Those of us wise enough knew to go to flowing water for our supplies, but a lot of the town relied on water stored in water butts, barrels or on beer made from still water. No one rightly knows how the contagion came in.'

'Yep, there it was,' said Vetters. 'We had the cholera in town, and men – and women too, who had come to work in the local brothel – fell like flies.'

'That was a hard time for me,' admitted King. 'I quarantined my family – Ben was only five at the time, and the youngest hadn't even been born.' The thought of what he had been saying dawned on him, and there was a brooding silence for half a minute until he regained control. 'I stayed away and tended those I could. These here men helped me out and we got rid of the dead as quickly as they piled up. I've had some medical training and I know that you have to get rid of the source of the infection as quickly as possible.'

'What he's saying is,' put in Sutton, 'that we got sick too, but not as sick as most, and we all recovered.'

'We got some kind of immunity,' said Vetters, 'big word, I know, but that's what John told us.'

The cholera epidemic had nearly been the undoing of the town. The rumours that Purgatory was a place of death had persisted, and had certainly put off a lot of potential explorers. Besides the decline in returns of gold and silver, and even lead, it also explained why so few people remained at the time of the raid by Valsquez and his men, with barely a hundred settlers left for him to capture for his nefarious purposes.

The girl was not entirely convinced, but could see that they were willing to risk staying overnight in the barn, and had nowhere else to go.

'But you'll have to leave as soon as you can in the morning,' she told them. 'When the men you killed don't return to their communities there will be others.'

She didn't say so, but King could see that their presence was a comfort to her.

He made sure that the bodies were taken away and hidden in the undergrowth, and then they all settled down for the night.

CHAPTER SIX

It was a raid, that's what it was, a raid for anything that could be gained, an early morning intrusion when it would be wise to get out as quickly as possible. The first thing to do was to get to the stables and saddle up a horse, get on with as much stealth as possible, and then get out – ride like hell and get into the nearest town, sell the horse and get to the railways – miles away from here – and go to the city. There was always a living to be made in Houston, people to be served, big houses looking for servants. A servant, yes, that would do, looking after others.

A pity about the theft, but it was a theft for a greater cause, the cause of self-preservation, and that was the greatest aim of all.

Opening one of the stalls, he led out one of the quieter horses, a big grey mare. Luckily the saddles had also been stored in the stables. He flung a blanket on the horse's back, put on the saddle and tightened the straps, working quickly and easily in the grey light of dawn. When you were used to doing this for others you became adept at doing it for yourself.

'Hey!' he was just getting on when the shout came from the direction of the one main building that was left, the barn.

He swung into the saddle, grabbed the reins and gave a sharp tug. Already two men, one of them big and broad, were running across to the stables. The biggest man didn't bother with any tack; he grabbed a big black gelding and jumped on its naked back, kicking its flanks with his heels, and took up the chase.

The second man followed the first and got on a chestnut stallion, also riding in this way, taking up the chase with his friend. Both of them were armed, but they had thrust their pistols into their waistbands when they had heard the disturbance outside.

Riding hard, the thief thundered along the dirt road that led out of the ranch and towards the woodlands beyond. He was not the most expert horseman, and had to slow down when he came to the bend in the road.

This was a signal for the big man behind him, who risked snatching out his pistol and taking a pot shot at the thief. The shot went wide, but the man in front jabbed his spurs into the side of his mount and the mare sprang forwards as if electrified.

The woodland trail was not as well defined as the dirt road, but the rider seemed to know where he was going and rode grimly forwards. If he kept riding like this he would soon be miles from the Hawkes spread and the area with which his pursuers were familiar. Then, he thought to himself, there was a good chance they would give up.

The only problem was, the biggest man who was trailing him had picked a big black gelding with plenty of stamina. He was starting to draw in front of his companion, leaving him behind.

'I don't want to shoot,' he yelled, 'but if you don't stop, I will.'

The rider being pursued realized he had made some kind of mistake. He sensed that his pursuers were not about to give up after all, but he spurred the mare onwards and she responded with one final burst of speed, and he lost sight of the other two in the trees. But it was obvious that his lead could not last, for the simple reason that his horse was tiring. She was sweating and trembling and her breath was becoming more labored.

A building came into sight, an old abandoned farm. A lot of settlers had come out here to start new lives, but the difficulty of clearing land, disease, and the many conflicts that had scarred this part of Texas had driven many away – but it was a godsend to him.

He brought the mare to a trembling halt and flung himself off the saddle and ran along what was left of the path, now mostly overgrown, and into the empty building. Just as he vanished, his pursuers arrived.

The man in the lead went over to the mare, took

her reins and comforted her with soft words for a few seconds until his companion joined him.

They could take their horse back and depart, but that would leave behind a possibly dangerous foe, who might shoot at them, taking their lives as they attempted to leave.

With a mutual nod they pulled out their guns and flanked the main door of the empty farmhouse.

It was quite a large building that had once held the hopes and dreams of a family of settlers. Now the interior had only a smell of decay and most of the furnishings were gone, long since taken away by local raiders.

The biggest man scanned the living area and saw nothing, then signalled for his friend to enter in a low voice.

'I think he's upstairs,' he said. This was dangerous – they had been right to enter, because the thief could have shot at them from an upper window.

'We're coming to get you!' said the smaller man, 'surrender!' There was a moment of silence, then a dark-clad figure came down the stairs, holding up its hands.

'Don't shoot me,' said the thief, 'please, they've killed all my family. Please.'

The voice was high-pitched, but it was not that of a girl or woman.

They were looking at a young boy of about thirteen years old.

CHAPTER SEVEN

Any questions were kept between the three of them until they got back to what had been the Hawkes' spread. They were met half way on their return by Vetters, who was fully armed and looked grim. Carter and King, who had been the pursuers, greeted him in a lighter vein as he stared at the dark-clad figure who rode a little behind them.

'It's all right, we're not going to harm this one,' said King, and they all returned to the barn where the girl stood, looking alarmed at what had been happening.

Being miners, and used to looking after their own needs in some extreme situations, they soon managed to catch some fish and rustle up some fruit and vegetables from the surrounding area, besides finding some meat from a storehouse, and they had brought their own basic utensils with them.

They sat down to a meal around the campfire just outside the barn. Given what had happened the

47

previous day, King didn't want to stay around too long, and as they ate he turned to the young man.

'What is your name?'

'I am Lucas,' said the boy. He had dark skin and very white teeth that flashed in his face as he spoke, and big brown eyes that gazed at them mournfully. He wore a dark grey tunic beneath his dark coat, had thrust his hat in his pocket, and had men's trousers made of worsted wool.

'What's your story?' asked King in a very direct way. He was not a man who had ever patronized or spoken down to young people. He always treated them as people he could reason with, expecting an honest response, and getting it a great deal more often than might have been expected.

'It was them,' said Lucas, his manner a little confused. 'The men, they came to us and they took over. They tried to use us as slaves, we fought back, and that is when they turned on us and killed some of us before we could run away.'

'There is a lot here I need to think about,' said King. 'Can I ask you where you were, where you lived?'

'It was a village,' said the young man, 'called Valensis, on the banks of the Brazos near the biggest bend in the river.'

'Wait a minute,' said Vetters, 'I know where he's talking about. Pa was in the civil war, I won't say what side he was on, but I remember him mentioning a place called Big Bend.'

'But why would they want to capture a little

village?' asked Sutton.

'I've heard of that place, too,' put in Carter.

'So have I,' said the girl, Alice, unexpectedly. 'It's where the woman came from with her baby, a good few miles away. They flung her out to protect themselves.' There was a bitter tone in her voice: by helping another person she had lost everything.

'That's a consideration,' said Carter, 'what if this boy hasn't been in contact with the disease, what if he catches it?'

'I was ill,' said the boy, 'long before the men came, and it was from the illness that all fear that my mother sheltered me, and made sure that it was hidden until I recovered, yes she sheltered me,' his eyes clouded over at the thought, and it was plain that he was thinking of one who was no longer with them.

'That's the thing,' said Carter, 'Big Bend was a place where they stationed men, ain't that right Vetters?'

'It was more than a place where men were stationed,' said Vetters, 'it was an actual fort, a big one too, called Fort Geffen. It was named after the commander of the division that was stationed there, Frank Geffen. This was way back when the tribes – especially the Kiowa and the Comanche – were still on the warpath, and the Mexicans were still smarting from the fact that the territory they had considered theirs had been taken over as part of Texas.'

'Hell, I can see why that would be the case,' said

Carter. 'We all learned this at our mama's knee, I guess, the state was formally constituted in '45. Just a few years before that Santa Anna and his men was fighting at the Alamo and the whole thing threatened to turn into a full-scale war.'

'It was far from the only fort,' said Vetters. 'From what I hear they had forts up and down the length of the Brazos. The heck with it, with the Mexican border being so close and then with the war, I guess it was a miracle that any Westerners ever colonized this part of the country at all.'

'But this is taking us away from the boy,' said King. 'What happened, son?'

'The *bandidos* – or so we thought they were – came to our village,' said the young man. 'We were much scared, but they were friendly at first, and their leader was recognized too, by some of our younger men, and he was treated like a hero.'

'Valsquez,' breathed King so softly they could barely hear him.

'Yes, yes, that was the name,' said Lucas. He looked around the assembled company. 'They wanted us to help them with the fort, a place we have used in many ways. It has a source of water, a deep well fed by the springs that go to the river, it has places for shelter, and it has given us stone for the walls of our homes.' He looked around for their attention, and saw that they were still intent on his words.

'What happened next was terrible. Our leaders were told that we must work on the fort, that it must be rebuilt. They had many more weapons than us. Some of our young men believed what they wanted must be done because the rebellion against the Americans must continue.' He paused again. 'My father was one of those who held out. He was killed, and so was my mother. I was told that I should have joined them, and I fled, I struggled to get away quickly in the countryside – which is why I stole your horse, sorry.'

They could all understand why a young man with so much on his mind might try to get as far away from his troubles as possible.

'You saw what they were doing?' asked King.

The young man thought about this for a little while, his head in his hands.

'No,' he said, 'No, I didn't see what they were doing, or why. I just know they want to rebuild.'

'Then it's a mystery,' said King, 'and one that we are going to solve.'

'What are you saying?' asked Lucas.

'I have to tell you this,' said King 'you must be very smart indeed to have made it this far.' The boy looked at the man who was a stranger to him as if he was being mocked, and decided that King was being serious.

'I know many ways,' he said, 'we would play in the hills and I learned all the places we could go.' King looked questioningly at Vetters, who gave a brief nod.

'The hills at the River Bend are well known,' said Vetters, 'they're part of the reason the fort was built there in the first place.'

'I don't understand,' said Carter.

'Well it's simple enough, with the fort being built higher than the surrounding countryside, they could look out a lot better for the enemy,' said Vetters, 'a position of strength, you might say.'

'Did your father tell you a lot about the fort?' asked King seriously.

'I guess he was a good old guy,' said Vetters. 'He married my mom late in his life, and he died when I was ten; he never got hurt bad and he loved to tell me his stories of the civil war. But the war was over long before I was born.'

'Any knowledge will be useful for us,' said King. 'The slightest thing you know could make a difference to the outcome. And we're not going to back down – well, at least not one of us.' He brought his attention back to bear on the boy. 'Lucas, are you going to help us?'

'What do you mean, sir?' asked the boy.

'You are going to have to be vigilant and helpful in what you do for us,' said King, 'but I want you to take us back to the village through the ways that you know.' He spoke in a firm voice, again not as one talking down to a child, but as to another adult.

'Sir,' Lucas looked up, and although there were no tears, his eyes were bright. 'I have suffered too much; I have gone away from that place because of what they have done. I can't go back – I can never go back – and you can't make me.'

CHAPTER EIGHT

Valsquez and the former aristocrat Hernandez rode into the village at the head of the stumbling column of people they had brought with them. The village of Valensis had been much larger before the border raids and disease had made many of the population flee, but already some of the buildings had been brought to the ground and reduced to rubble as part of a deliberate policy of destruction on the part of those who had decided on the method of their rebellion.

This might have seemed like a simple act of vandalism on the part of the invading forces, the buildings – some of them two storeys high – having been brought down to piles of rubble by big battering rams made out of pinc trees cut down and stripped of their branches, some of which lay nearby. It was quite clear that the destruction had been systematic and deliberate, and no invading force would waste their energy in this way to no purpose. They would not want to destroy the fabric of the village, especially when it was obvious that the invaders were far outnumbered by those they held captive.

Valsquez held up an imperious hand and the column of men and some women behind him were brought to an abrupt halt by their captors. He turned in the saddle, an impressive figure in his gold-trimmed uniform.

'This is where you have been brought to do the great work. You will be treated well as long as you do what is asked. There is plenty of water. The food will have to be rationed, and there is little in the way of fresh bread, but we will feed you and make sure you have shelter.'

'Jorge,' said Hernandez quietly, still on his big horse and speaking in a low voice, 'why be merciful? These are just filthy animals, pawns in what we must do for the good of our land.'

Valsquez turned back to his second-in-command and gave him a seemingly benign look, and spoke rapidly in Spanish.

'Victor, I know what you think of the gringo, and in some ways I share your views. But the worse we treat these people the worse it will be for us. We have a mission and we must keep them well enough to do the great work.' He pulled on the reins and turned his horse towards the former inhabitants of Purgatory. 'I will let you rest for a period of one hour, you will have water and some food, and then you will continue with the good work. My men will make sure that you are looked after. But I warn you, if any one of you tries to escape, they will not survive – so it is better to follow orders. Señor Hernandez is your leader from now on; I have other work to do. But you will all be with me shortly.' Then he turned and saluted Hernandez, who saluted back, then rode off without looking back.

Hernandez looked over the hundred or so people who had been pushed and cajoled into a motley assembly in what had once been the village, the buildings on two sides reduced to their constituent parts.

'You see those stones around you? They were stolen, stolen by the witless and used to make their own homes, an inn here and there, or a shop. You are here to take those stones back to where they rightly belong, and you will toil for many hours each day because you have a great and glorious task.' His voice grew blurry with triumph: 'Look up,' he said, 'look high, for this is your work.'

Over a hundred heads lifted and looked, their eyes resting on the hills above the village where lurked a structure of stones so big and grey that it blended in with the greys and greens surrounding it. Maybe they had been expecting a building where forty or so troops had been garrisoned during the Civil War, or perhaps a semi-structure, a total ruin.

What many did not know was that the Big Bend of the Brazos had been a strategic location during the Civil War, so any fort constructed there had a high importance for the commanders of that war.

Fort Geffen was so big, and fitted in so well with

the rolling hills overlooking the river that it was hard to take in with one look, but they were close enough to see that some of the walls had a ruinous look that could not have been caused by mere wind and weather in the thirty or so years since the war had ended. They could even see that the wall nearest the village was almost totally gone.

'Your amigos left this place,' said Hernandez, 'when they thought they were the conquerors, and they no longer needed that which they had used to oppress us. Now feed and rest for the good work begins soon.'

As usual the women were seconded to the task, and in clear sight of the troops, the food was taken from where it was stored and handed out. The so-called 'meal' consisted of a little bit of long-baked bread that had gone so hard it was almost impossible to chew, some corn, and a scrap of meat that could have been hidden when a man closed his fist.

For all that they were grateful for what they had been given, and ate it as fast as they could. Most of them had eaten very little since their captivity, and the enforced march had taxed their bodies to the limit.

The soldiers were fed a little more than their captives. They were mostly dark men who had no hesitation in guarding their prisoners, eating in turns so that any signs of rebellion could be swiftly suppressed. The guards were dressed in grey uniforms that were already showing some kind of wear and tear. The hats were black, flat at the top and padded, coming down over their ears, and they wore a tunic with long sleeves.

They were mostly young, some of them little above fifteen years old, and they had the cruel indifference of youth to the suffering of others. They were fit and strong and could subsist on what they were given, so why couldn't the prisoners?

The hour that Hernandez had promised was over all too quickly, and the men and women were ordered to their feet in the village square. Ben was still amongst these people who had once been his neighbours. He could not exactly say they had been his friends because his father had protected his children from the worst excesses of the town, keeping them apart in a slightly self-conscious way. He had done this not because they were 'better' as he reminded them, but because they would be leaving soon for a proper life in one of the big cities.

Hernandez looked at the assembled men and women with eyes like those of a dead fish.

'Get to work now, and we don't stop until night-fall.'

That was when Jonathan Boscoe stepped forward. Boscoe had been something of a firebrand in the town, always arguing for improvements. It was as if he had owned the town in some manner. Like many of the miners, he was a small, wiry man who sprouted an impressive beard that made him look much older than his thirty years. Like the others, dragooned as he had been out of his home and made to march, he had been too swept up in

57

the tide of what had happened to protest, especially with the cold and lethargy of the morning. Now he felt a little more empowered to speak.

'Say, mister, this is a liberty, don't you realize what you're doing?'

'What am I doing?' asked Hernandez. There was a thin-lipped smile on his face as he sat on his stallion before the man.

'You're doing something you shouldn't,' said Boscoe in a positive way. He had often let forth like this at town meetings. 'You took us from our homes and brought us to this durned place, and now you're makin' slaves of us all.' He turned his back to the new commander and addressed the assembled crowd. Ben, who was standing at the front, felt a sudden chill running though his veins. 'Don't let them treat us like this any more. Face up to the bastards; refuse to do what they say. We outnumber them five to one, come on, who's with me?'

His words had an effect. The people of Purgatory had rested; they had lost that edge of exhaustion and the air of hopelessness that had overcome them since being taken into captivity.

'He's right,' shouted out someone from the crowd. 'We ain't prisoners.'

'Listen up,' Boscoe turned around and faced Hernandez again. 'These are citizens of this here state, when the governor gets to know of this here outrage there'll be hell to pay and you'll be the ones who suffer. The more you do here, the worse it will be for you and your men.'

'I see, well, can I ask you what your name is, my friend?' asked Hernandez. He had to speak up because there was a swelling anger going through the captives that could well get out of control within seconds.

'Name's Boscoe,' said the miner.

'Very well, here's your reply, Mister Boscoe,' said Hernandez. He pulled a gun out of his waistband and fired at point-blank range, the noise making his stallion whinny and shift uneasily on the cobbled square. A hole appeared in Boscoe's forehead and the bullet passed right through the back of his head. The body stood there for a moment, then fell backwards into its own gore.

There was a tense moment when the assembled people could have gone either way. Their anger and total rage could have swept them over a precipice where they would have risked all, weaponless though they were. But Hernandez was prepared for that too: he gave a sharp command in Spanish and the rifles were at the ready. His men would fall fighting, and they were quite prepared to die for the cause they believed in.

Then the moment of possible rebellion passed and would never happen again, because from that point on the prisoners would not be assembled in quite the same way.

'Let the work begin,' said Hernandez, with not a glimmer of a smile. He looked at the corpse that lay before him. 'And get this out of the way.' He focused his gaze on Ben, 'You look young and strong; you and the woman beside you throw it into the bushes and get on with your work.'

Ben swallowed hard as he helped Lillian, the woman who had once been a prostitute, drag away the dead man. Once again, he knew that given the slightest chance he was going to take his revenge for the indignities heaped upon his people.

The one hour respite was nothing to what the men and women of Purgatory had to endure. The village had a couple of carts. These were old-fashioned, low-sided wagons that had mostly been used for transporting animal feeds to the fields beyond the village. Now they were used for a very different purpose indeed. Each cart had a team of horses hitched to it, and the new arrivals were forced to fill one of the carts with stone.

Ben was given no quarter – he worked with the rest, and soon there was a pile of stones in the cart that could have made a small outbuilding. The cart took off and headed for the fort, groaning under the weight of its load.

The many-tailed whip was used again, and a hopeless line of people made to follow after. They, too, were carrying stones.

CHAPTER NINE

Lucas got up from where they were sitting, trembling all over like a young colt.

'You don't know what it was like, I can't go back there.'

'I understand,' said King. If he had shouted at the boy Lucas would have departed there and then, but instead he stood his ground.

'You don't know,' said Lucas, 'I can't go, I really can't. I saw them kill those I loved. I have to go to town. In another year I'll fill out, be a man, my voice'll change. I'll get work on a farm, or the railroad. I've always loved trains. I can't go back. Besides, we'd been planning to leave, my family I mean. After the disease the village seemed doomed, and that big fort hanging over us, it just seemed like a cursed place.'

'And how will you get to the nearest town?' asked King.

'I'll walk,' said Lucas, thrusting out his young jaw and curling his fists.

'Alice,' asked King, 'if Lucas leaves us, will you let him have one of your horses? He can't have the grey mare, Meg, she belonged to my wife.'

'He can have one of the horses,' she said, a faint bitterness creeping into her voice, 'what good are they to me, anyway?'

'I'm grateful to you sir, and madam,' said the young man looking from one person to the other.

'Your local knowledge would have been invaluable,' said King. 'But I can't turn from my task, and neither can these men or this young woman. And even if they did, I would still go on.'

'Why, why would you do such a foolish thing?' asked the young man.

'They destroyed *my* family,' said King simply, 'and they have my only remaining son, a boy just a few years younger than you. They have many people I looked after for years. I was a kind of doctor in my time in Purgatory. If I give up now I'll be betraying not just my wife, God bless her, but also my son and those people.'

'I am sorry for that,' said Lucas, 'but none of that is my fault, and I have to protect what I have left.'

'You're right,' said the leader, 'because there is no right and wrong here, only choices. Come on, I'll help you pick a horse.' He looked around at the assembled company '. . . and I guess that goes for all of us. Looks like the guys of certain extraction around here are getting pretty restless. Time we got away from here and into the wild.' Sutton, Vetters and Carter all got up and smothered the remains of the camp fire to avoid the risk of embers blowing over and setting fire to the barn; also the smoke would attract more attention to the area.

Alice was quite happy with this. She went back into the barn to make sure that no stray embers from the fire had got into the hay. Satisfied that this was the case, she turned to find that she was not alone. Carter had followed her inside, and there was a strange expression on his face, watchful, and half tender.

'I still own this place, I guess,' she said, 'and I'll want to be coming back here when this is all over and make something of what's left.'

'You would need help of some kind,' said Carter, looking straight at her.

'Well, maybe someone would be willing to stay on and work with me, with what I have to do.' She gave a deep sigh. 'Already thinking of moving on, I feel as if I'm not respecting my parents.'

'The only way you would fail to respect them would be if you gave up,' said Carter. By this time the others had moved away to get ready, and she suddenly found a strong pair of arms around her as he held her close. Then abruptly he let her go and she stepped back, her eyes wide.

'I'm sorry, ma'am. I don't know what came over me.'

'Let's help out the rest,' she said, 'things don't

get ready on their own.' He followed her out of the barn, somehow, despite his size, the smaller of the two.

King said nothing as he made sure that one of the fresher animals, a big brown quarter horse, was made ready for the boy. He checked that the under blanket was in place, and that the saddle and reins were secure. As they did this, Vetters appeared at the door of the stables.

'You ain't letting this one go, are you?' he asked with a look of withering scorn that made Lucas shrink a little.

'This young man has seen some terrible things in his time,' said King, 'we're not the kind of people to take away his liberty. It's his choice if he wants to come with us.'

'I don't understand you,' said Vetters, but he now wore a look of respect for the man who had become his leader.

Lucas was soon on the back of the horse, and looked down at the man who had assisted him.

'If you go north you'll come to a trading post,' said King. 'Tell them who sent you; they might even give you a job.'

The young man looked as if he was going to say something, but he could hardly speak. He nodded his head, spurred his horse forwards and departed.

But one cartful of stones was not the end for the captives. The cart was brought down and loaded again and they were given grain sacks, baskets and

anything else that might act as a carry-all, and
forced to walk to the fort, each one carrying his or
her burden.

Ben, though, had a completely different experience. The second, empty cart was halted before
him, and along with a big man called Helmuth, a
taciturn German who had been a relentless miner,
he was made to climb on the back. They had broad
shovels thrown in with them. On board the cart
were several wooden barrels that took up most of
the space. Two guards accompanied them, one
steering the cart and the other guarding them with
a Winchester rifle.

Instead of heading for the fort they were taken
down to the banks of the Brazos quite a distance
from the actual village itself. Ben tried hard to
imagine why they were being taken there, but even
he was surprised by the result.

Big Bend was at a part of the Brazos where the
river widened out considerably as it followed the
contours of the land. Because it was in a giant
curve the river had actually created its own estuary,
and the banks were wide and subject to tidal
changes.

This meant there was an area that had been considerably flattened, creating huge reserves of thick
mud on a wide beach.

'Get off,' said the guard, pulling the back of the
cart down and forcing them out with a gesture of
his weapon and the threat of death. 'You two, you
dig. You dig as well,' he added speaking to the

driver who looked indignant at the thought and helped them in a desultory fashion.

'But what's it for?' asked Ben still curious about what they were doing there.

'Quiet!' said the guard and cuffed his ears for daring to speak. Ben felt the sting and glowered with anger, but he still had a rifle pointing at him, and he began to dig.

In his mind he had always thought of mud as soft brown stuff that could be flung around with ease, but what he was digging now seemed to be of another kind of substance altogether – it was thick, gritty, glutinous, and hard to dig, and it stank of decay from all the millions of marine creatures that had died in it.

The barrels seemed to take forever to fill, and Helmuth, big and taciturn as ever, set to work with a will. He did not understand much of what had happened to them, but he understood how to dig, since it had been his only occupation for years as he searched for precious metals.

Once the barrels were filled they were rolled back on to the cart via boards especially set up for that purpose, then the men climbed aboard and the whole company headed towards Fort Geffen.

As they came closer to this huge formation, Ben saw that the fort had wide, strengthened gates constructed of solid strips of white oak joined with iron strips. These were gates that any invader would have major difficulty breaking open. The way to the fort was along a military road that was still in surprisingly good condition this long after the civil war. The gates were useless because to each side the walls were largely missing, which was the reason for the presence of the enslaved people.

As they climbed up the hill and passed between the open gates Ben finally saw what the mud was for. Men from the village were creating a mortar made from the mud and some yellowish powder that had an acrid smell. Ben had seen this substance before: it was called quicklime and was used in building work. The mortar was being made just a few feet from where it was going to be used.

The barrels were immediately seized upon their arrival, and the mud was poured out and mixed with the quicklime to create a kind of cement, which when dried would be as solid as anything that held together the capitol building in Houston. Ben was set to work mixing with the rest, but he was careful enough not to get the acrid powder on his clothes or his feet, and he tied a cloth 'kerchief across his face so that he did not breathe in the dust. Many others did the same.

Other villagers were starting to put the walls back together, working with a speed that seemed terrifying to Ben. Heaps of stones purloined from the village lay to either side, and it was obvious that this was the sole purpose of bringing them there.

Once the mortar had been mixed, the stones

were put in place by men who obviously knew what they were doing. Hernandez supervised the work and he made sure that the stones were laid in roughly straight lines.

Unfortunately it was impossible to make progress as quickly as he wanted. The risk was that if too many of the grey stones were piled atop each other before the cement had set properly, all their work would be undone. As it was, at measured intervals the new part of the wall was being supported by roughly stripped lengths of pine, the same as the battering rams that had been used to destroy the buildings down below.

For Ben it was a relief when he was pulled away from his task, because he was hungry and thirsty. He was sent back down to the village under guard to help garner more of the stone that was being used to restore the walls of the building.

There was some recognition of his plight, because he was given a drink of water from a stone jar when this was requested. Hernandez was not stupid enough to think that he could make his captives work for much longer without drinking. Ben supped on the water offered for a long time. He was ravenous, but food was a different matter.

'None,' said the guard when asked, 'none yet, gringo.'

Then the boy was set to work again, struggling manfully to load yet another cart and carrying stones on his back up to a fort where the need for such a measure never seemed to diminish, while his body ached at every level from the bottom of his soles to the top of his head.

The walls on either side had grown steadily since their arrival that morning, and the sun was high in the sky, drying the cement fast.

Not long after, the thirst returned.

CHAPTER TEN

The four men rode towards the hills that stood in front of the mighty River Brazos, which had so long been a mark of division between the two countries. Vetter was taking the lead now, based on the knowledge that he had gleaned from his dead father. King was wise enough to let another show the way if they had more knowledge than he did of what they were doing.

'As far as I know,' he said, 'there's a whole lot of hills, quite a bit of woodland, and part of the old cattle trail near Fort Geffen. Hell, I don't really know much else,' said Vetters.

'I think it would surprise you,' said King. 'Some knowledge is better than none, and yours is all we have to go on.'

This might have been the case at that precise moment, a couple of miles away from the Hawkes' burned out ranch, where the woodland gave way to brush country, and where the hills were visible in the middle distance – but there was an interruption.

'I can hear the sound of a horse's hoofs,' said the girl. Anyone who was riding fast towards them could only be doing so for a reason, to intercept them, and in these dangerous times that reason might not be with kind intentions. They turned and faced the sound of the new arrivals, guns in hand.

One rider burst out of the woodland, crouching low in the saddle as he urged his horse forwards. It was Lucas, and the expression on his face told them everything. He brought his steed to a halt before them as they put away their weapons.

'Señor King, I thought of what you said about your family, how they died and you go to save them. The thought preyed on my mind, and I asked the Virgin what I should do, and now I am here,' he said simply. King was not the kind of man to make a fuss; he simply gave a kindly, weary smile.

'Thank you,' he said, 'you have done well, son.'

The six rode onwards, with their leader keen to get them away from open country and out towards the hills that surrounded the fort where they could see evergreen woodland and growths of oak and cedar.

Vetters seemed a little put out by the return of their young friend, but King was clever enough to know what was happening and he waited to speak to the miner, who was trailing behind now.

'Listen to me, Will, you know a little about the

71

fort and that's going to make all the difference when we get there – believe you me, even a little knowledge will allow us to get in there and do what has to be done. But that young guy has lived in the village all his life, he has roamed those hills and he knows them in a way we can't. You're as valuable as he is.'

'Yeah, well I don't like getting involved with any greaser,' said Vetters, 'not after what they done to our people.'

'Do you know what?' asked King rhetorically, 'that's what keeps people divided. That boy has lost his loved ones. You lost some friends, sure, but he's come back because he's recognized that the only way to get some closure is to face up to what's happened. Know something else? In some ways this might be for nothing, we might be captured and killed, but at least we'll have tried.'

Will Vetters did not say anything to this, but as he joined the main body he was looking noticeably more cheerful and he looked at the young man who had rejoined them without further rancour.

As always, when things are in the distance the hills looked much closer than they were. One piece of knowledge King gleaned from their companion was that these were known as the Pinto hills and had once been the domain of the Comanche when they were fighting the cavalry and the hiding point for bandits, who could use their presence here to branch out into other counties. It was with a sense of relief that they arrived in the shelter of more woodland.

'Do you know where we are, Lucas?' asked King.

'*Sí, señor*, we are at the back of Fort Geffen, where it faces on to the River Brazos,' said Lucas. 'My village is to the left of here, and to the right are more Pinto hills and caves.'

'This used to be Indian Territory,' said Carter, 'I remember that lore from when I was little. They hid out around here and fought the Cavalry for years before they were brought to heel.'

King said nothing to this. To him it felt as if the boot was distinctly getting put on the other foot. Like many of those who had come to Texas for the opportunities offered by such a big country, he had never really given much thought to what the natives had endured so that this land could be opened up by the Westerners. There was one thing he did know about the natives, though, they had held out for many years, which must mean that this land was an easy place in which to live and hide for unspecified periods of time – and he wanted to be here with his men for enough time to do what they wanted.

'You said we could find some caves or hollows around here?' he asked.

'*Sí señor*, they are a short ride away.' said Lucas. 'We used them when we were exploring, if the night came on when we were out we would shelter there instead of trying to get home in the dark. My mama would scold me.' Here he broke off as he mentioned his mother, and once more it was brought home to King that they were dealing with a young man barely into his teenage years.

There was, however, no time for a great deal of emotion.

'Let's get out of here,' said King, 'at least we have somewhere to go.'

'Even more news,' said Vetters, 'from what I hear the Brazos ain't too fussy about where it goes, there's all sorts of underground streams and things, so there will be plenty of water and game for our needs.' A thoughtful expression came over his face at his own words, but his thoughts were interrupted by King.

'What would be one of the first things you would do if you were defending a fort?'

'You would set up lookouts,' said Sutton.

'Which is why we have to get out of here,' said King. 'Lucas, you take the lead.' The young man did not need any encouragement, and he took them away from the rocky escarpment they had been facing, and led them to a place he knew well.

King could see why this must have been a great locality for a young man and his companions when they were learning to hunt. The land around was useless for farming because it was so uneven, the trail was not well marked, and there were sudden ascents and descents that made their progress slower than it could have been.

They reached the area they were looking for within about half an hour. By this time they had all been on the trail for hours, the horses were growing

74

tired, and there was a distinct need for regrouping. The only reason King had pushed them onwards was the thought that they might have been observed from the back of the fort. However, he hadn't seen any sentries, and nor had any of the others – but that didn't mean they weren't there.

After one particularly steep descent, they found themselves at a part of the land where there was a natural split in the hills caused by many years of erosion by a tributary of the main river. The area was green, with many beech and oak trees growing on the banks of the water.

'Good hunting ground,' said Lucas. 'This is where many of the animals come to drink, especially in the summer when the plains are dry and dusty.'

There was a green and pleasant air about the place. Indeed, some deer fled when they arrived and they could hear woodpeckers tapping in the trees, while other birds sang their territorial songs. The temptation was to linger in this pleasant spot beside the softly flowing waters. The winter rains had not yet arrived and the river was low and easy to cross, as it barely flowed over the rocky bed beneath.

King put their unspoken thoughts into words.

'No, we're not staying here, because if we do we'll be clearly visible to anyone who comes along, and who's to say that Valsquez hasn't already sent out hunting parties for food? He has a lot of mouths to feed.'

This was so patently true that tired though they were, they had to continue onwards – indeed Alice had been about to make that very suggestion about staying there, as was evidenced by the way she closed her mouth and looked at the ground.

Arriving at a low banking they dismounted from their horses and elected to walk with them across the river. Although the waters were low, this was the best way to get across because the riverbed was uneven, and one slip with a fall against an exposed rock could be fatal.

Once across they found themselves in a place of gloomy green. The hills seemed to hang over them like an old man bending to pick something up, and this, combined with the greenery, meant that they were in a kind of open valley, if there could be such a thing.

'We're there,' said Lucas in triumph. 'The good hiding places are forward from here, between the hills.'

'I guess I owe you an apology,' said Vetters. They were still walking as they led their horses to the gap between the hills. 'I thought you might be treacherous, leading us here for your own ends.'

'Yeah, I sure had some problem with trust,' said Sutton, 'after what that bastard Valsquez did to our people, but I guess you ain't so bad, kid.'

'We have to trust someone,' said King, but he was smiling with relief. Soon they would find shelter, and be able to rest.

But at that very instant three figures, all armed

with Henry rifles and dressed in loose garments and wearing straw peasant hats, appeared in the pass.

CHAPTER ELEVEN

Valsquez was out again. He had disappeared into the recesses of the fort, but now he was walking along the lines of the walls and was nodding approvingly. Not that he was able to see a huge amount of detail, because the light had faded fast and it was almost dark. Those who had arrived that day had toiled without respite from their arrival until it was almost dark. One of his soldiers held a lighted torch, and Hernandez was by his side as he inspected the day's labour.

'How long do you think it will be now, Victor?' he asked his companion.

'The west wall is almost done,' said Hernandez, 'but the southern wall is a little more trouble. It used more material because it was more exposed.'

'But what is your estimate?'

'I would say at least another two days at the most.'

'Two days? It is still too long, but I am impressed – I never thought our little act of insurrection was going to happen at all, at one point.'

'That is true,' Hernandez gave a grimace. 'The problem was we were attacking Valensis itself, a place where the locals know the lie of the land so well that most of them managed to escape into the hills. And that was after the population had already been depleted by disease.'

'It is so,' Valsquez gave a grimace as he remembered their initial foray into revolution. 'But I have given orders that any peasant who is seen after this on our hunting trips is offered a choice: either they come into our glorious cause with us, or they will be summarily executed. There is no other way; they are either with us or against us.' He walked onwards inspecting the walls for a little longer.

They certainly were an impressive sight – the one that Ben had been working on earlier was now so high that ladders were needed to get to the top to continue the brickwork. Only another two layers were needed and it would be finished. The other wall was high, too. The new mortar was a grey colour, but here and there was a yellow tinge as the minerals embedded in it showed in the torchlight. Valsquez took out a dagger – he always carried one in his belt – and gave the mortar an experimental dig. There was the satisfying sound of his knife ringing off the material as if it had hit solid stone.

'Good work, Jorge! I am no expert, but from what I see this will withstand much.' He disappeared back into the building from where he had come, with his second-in-command behind.

The workers were herded away now into one of

the barracks that had once been the province of the soldiers who had been stationed at Fort Geffen. In common with the rest of the fort the barracks were huge, covering a large amount of the space inside the fort. The buildings had been constructed out of local materials, and unlike the walls of the fort, they were mostly intact, although the action of wind and weather had made the roof fall in here and there.

The wooden cots on which the soldiers would have slept were gone, and people had to bed down in the corners and around the edges of the barrack rooms. There was very little in the way of coverings for those who were so summarily herded together, and once they were made to go inside, the doors were locked so they couldn't escape. Not that most of them wanted to do anything like this in their exhausted condition. The strangest thing of all to Ben was that most of the women were gone – they had been taken elsewhere, and he couldn't fathom why, although one or two of them managed to fight back and refused to go even in their exhausted condition.

With little or nothing in the way of blankets and nothing much in the way of food, Ben felt cold and more tired than he had ever been in his life. One of the older women and big Helmuth huddled together with him for warmth. Ben had a sudden thought that cheered him up.

'This isn't the end,' he said. 'I know it isn't. My father knows I'm here and he's coming to get me.' The woman, whose name was Mags and who had been the 'Madame' of the town bordello, stroked his forehead with tenderness.

'I would have had a boy like you, except he died of the fever several years ago. Hush now and rest boy, we have to protect ourselves. The truth is, your father is dead, I saw your home reduced to rubble by a flying bomb.'

Her voice broke off. What little light there had been was gone now, and the prisoners sat there in the darkness, many of them falling asleep instantly through sheer exhaustion, while others called out and cursed their captors aloud.

The night crept on, and Ben's companions soon fell asleep too, because they had been worked as hard as the rest. Ben, though, lay there for a long time with his eyes open. There was a hole in the roof not far from where he lay huddled with the rest, and he saw the cold moon rising and the clouds that scuttled across the sky. He knew, somehow, that his father was out there, and he knew his father, too. John King was a remarkable man who had somehow shielded his family from the worst excesses of a remote mining town, who was loved and respected by all, and he never gave up.

Ben finally closed his eyes and slept, with inner warmth telling him that he was not alone.

CHAPTER TWELVE

The encounter would have turned into a bloodbath if it had not been for Lucas. The four men he was with were all armed, but they were exhausted, their nerves jangling from the long journey from Hawkes' ranch – men, moreover, who were expecting to fight for their lives at some point. Those confronting them, on the other hand, were alert and defensive for extremely good reasons of their own. Lucas jumped off his horse – no mean feat on that uneven ground – and stumbled towards them.

'Cousins, it is me.'

'Hold your fire,' said King, who held a Colt .45 in his right hand as he steadied his horse by the reins with the other.

'It's all right,' said Lucas to the young men who had appeared from the pass, 'these are friends of mine.' The two groups looked at each other suspiciously, and it was clear that there was still some degree of mistrust between them, but the presence of Lucas as a spokesman had done a lot to diffuse the tension. King and his men got off their horses and led those forwards, with the pack animals moving behind.

'These are Quinto, Juan and Riaz,' said Lucas. 'They are my cousins; I didn't know they had managed to escape. These are my friends,' he said to his cousins and introduced the former miners.

'Who are these people?' asked Quinto fiercely. He was a good-looking young man, about eighteen years of age, and it was plain from the look on his face that he distrusted the new arrivals.

'They are travellers in need of help,' said Lucas. 'And they are enemies of the insurrectionists.'

Quinto and companions glared fiercely at the new arrivals for a few seconds, while King looked him straight in the eye, then his expression relaxed.

'Very well, an enemy of theirs is an enemy of mine,' he said.

'This is all very well,' said King who had an eye for strategy, 'but I think we need to confine our introductions to the basics and get the hell out of here. Alice, you walk beside me.' He had noticed that the girl was looking a little frightened at the presence of so many people like the ones who had burned down the ranch, and he could understand why.

If Lucas was a traitor, this was the moment when his true treachery would have been revealed, and they would find themselves prisoners of the very people they were trying to fight, so they went into the mountain pass with their hands over their weapons.

King understood at once why the Comanche had given the cavalry such a hard time in this area. The land between the hills was so uneven that it was hard for horses to move along. The area split into a series of green hills and escarpments that were good for hiding people. They could have been surrounded by a hundred men without knowing they were there.

Finally Quinto led them to a space between the rocks that brought them to where there was an encampment. The space broadened out, and somehow he and his companions had managed to get together some 'A' tents, and had built other shelters out of brushwood. Signs showed that they had built fires, burning more brushwood to keep warm in the long cold nights and for cooking the food they had caught during their retreat from the village. The camp looked distinctly deserted. Quinto stood in the hollow and looked around with dark eyes.

'It's all right,' he said in a low but penetrating voice, and soon, from the surrounding area, at least twenty people appeared, most of them belonging to an age group below thirty.

King stood and looked at the assembled people.

'Well,' he said, 'I never expected this.'

It was Quinto who told the story as they sat in front of a low fire that had been deliberately set alight beneath one of the rocky overhangs that dominated the hollow land and where they had hidden themselves from Valsquez and his men. The

84

overhang deflected the smoke downwards and dif-
fused it into the bushes around them. King and his
companions were seated around the fire, while
Alice was the object of attention for the few young
women who were there.

'They came, Valsquez, Hernandez and their men.
They pretended they were there to trade with us,
but we knew them for what they were: they are
Abolitionists.'

'I have heard of Valsquez' reputation,' said King.
'He wants to restore the rule of Mexico in these
lands and take them back to what they were.'

'The Abolitionists lived amongst us for a short
while and tried to recruit some of us.' Quinto
looked directly at King as he said this, and King
had the strange feeling that the young man had
been considering becoming part of what was fast
becoming some kind of insurrection against the
state.

'This never happened,' he said. 'Disease had
come to our village not long before, carrying off a
lot of young people and the old. Those who were
left just wanted to get on with life, we had no place
for his type. That was when he turned against us.
But along with my brothers I managed to rouse the
village. We took what we could from our own village
and fled like thieves in the night.'

'But why would he turn against you?' asked King.

'Because we would not do his bidding,' said
Quinto. 'He made it obvious after a short while that
he wanted us to restore the fort, and we did not

want to do this.'

'Why not?'

'For many reasons, because life is hard enough without doing restoration work, because our numbers were so far reduced, and because we are not his slaves.'

'I can see that as a good reason.'

'But the worst part of all is that if we did such a thing we would be committing treason. We are part of America now, America is our country, and has been since our birth. We don't want to be part of Mexico.'

King made a snap decision at that point. He looked at his companions and said:

'Ant, Will, Jos, these people have every reason to hate the invaders and what has happened to their village. This looks as if it has no reason to become your fight any more, so if you want to leave I won't blame you.' King looked Quinto in the eye. 'Do you want to fight back, to stop them from continuing with this façade, to bring you back to the land you no longer want to be part of?'

'We cannot,' said Quinto. 'We have these old rifles,' he half lifted his Henry to show what he was talking about, 'but they are just for our defence. We have nothing else, and few bullets.'

'We have weapons,' said King, his voice stark and his tone grim, 'and we will use them with your help, if you so desire.'

'As for what you said,' Carter looked around. 'We're here now, I guess it's our fight too.'

Less than an hour later seven people were looking out from a vantage point that displayed Fort Geffen to them. One was Quinto, who of all the people who had fled seemed to have the makings of a leader. Alice was there too, having refused to stay in the hollow with the refugees and resolutely sticking with Carter. They were at a wooded hill that overlooked the fort, which lay to the east of where they stood, and because of the height of the hill they were looking slightly down on Fort Geffen. It was not a great vantage point for many reasons, but mainly because the fort was quite far away so it was hard to see a great deal of detail.

'I don't want us to get any closer,' said Quinto, speaking in a hushed voice. 'It is for the same reason that we are hiding here in the trees and bushes. If they see us they will kill or capture us. They are certain they are in the right, and that makes them fierce enemies.'

'Luckily I thought of this,' said King. He took a brass object out of his backpack. 'I thought we might have to study the lie of the land, and like you, my friend, I have an aversion to being caught or shot.' He pulled at the end of the instrument and the brass telescope opened as he put it to his eye.

'I don't need that thing to see what's happening,' said Vetters. 'My dad told me Fort Geffen was a bit of a ruin, but look at it, they've been building it back up. They're working on the walls right now.'

King said nothing, but scanned the area rapidly with his spyglass. It was much later in the day, because after their long trip they had all been exhausted and had had to rest. One of them had stayed on guard while the others slept for a couple of hours, and then he, too, had slept in turn. It was not that they particularly distrusted their new companions – most of who, once they understood what was going on, looked on them as liberators – but because they had a lot at stake and they were not taking any chances. For the same reason they had slept with their guns at their side.

'I don't see Ben,' he said, 'but look at this.' He handed the glass to Vetters who had a good look, passing it to Sutton and then to Carter. Lucas had a look too.

'I see people I worked with and helped every day toiling and breaking their backs to put up that damned wall,' said Carter in a flat voice that was somehow more frightening than pure anger.

'There are guards with whips and guns,' said Lucas, 'and my friends are there. They are so thin and frightened. They thought they were joining a cause and instead they are slaves.'

'They're getting the stone from the village,' continued King, who had taken the spyglass back and was doing a general sweep of the area. 'And I think I see Ben. It's hard to tell because he's dirty and far away, but the boy I see is about the right age.' His voice shook as he said the words.

'Once the walls are finished they'll lock the gates,'

said Carter, 'and it'll be like a fort of old – they'll be invincible, and no amount of the firepower we have will get them out.'

'Something I've noticed,' said Sutton, 'is that they don't have a hell of a lot of men; the guards are strung out pretty thin. If the gates are closed they'll have a great defence from fire power, as you say Carter.'

'He's right, they're strung out and have no great defence from the outside,' agreed King. 'Well, now we have to go back to camp and prepare for the worst that they can throw at us.'

They left then because there was nothing else they could do, but at least they had a sense of what they were up against.

Once they were back at the camp they sat with those who had fled from the scene and started to outline some plans for what could be done.

'You know,' Sutton said to Vetters, 'you told me something about Fort Geffen a whiles ago, Will, that might be useful.'

'And what was that?' Vetters was interested, and so were the rest because any information about the fort might be useful, no matter how trivial it might seem at the time.

'You said they had their own waste systems, ain't that right, and a well that drew in fresh water?'

'Yeah, I remember the old man telling me that. When the fort was built they designed it so they could stay inside for a good long whiles, keeping out hostiles like Mexes and Comanches. The commander had noticed that other forts that lacked that kind of thing fell a lot faster because their water supplies was cut off.'

'Don't rightly know how that helps us,' said Carter.

'It's just that Valsquez and his men might not know these things,' persisted Sutton. 'Could this be a possible way in?'

'You know what, I think that's a good avenue to explore,' said King. Lucas, who was sat nearby, was looking pale and thoughtful. King was not paying much attention to anything. It was later in the day and he had been impatient since his arrival, only giving half an hour to the meeting.

'I'm going for a ride,' said King as he stood up, brushing off his trousers. 'I have to clear my head.'

'Ain't you going to stay here and work out plans?' asked Carter.

'Jos, I'll let the five of you talk about what we should do, and I'll mull the same thing over. I need to do this.'

Carter grunted in agreement. He was big and slow-moving, but he had an agile mind, which is why he had lasted so long in Purgatory, and that's why he knew the value of solitude. They had been walking to get to the vantage point about half a mile away, because there was no way they could get horses that high. King fetched his dappled mare, the horse he had given to his wife what seemed an eternity ago, and took her out of the mountain pass. He rode off once he was outside the pass, going slowly over the uneven ground with a brooding look in his eyes that indeed indicated he was hatching some kind of plan.

CHAPTER THIRTEEN

Ben felt as if his old life had been a dream. He was still hungry, but once more they had been fed barely a scrap of food for breakfast. When he had woken that morning he had been cold and stiff, and had moved away from Mags' arms and had walked up and down, his circulation soon restored by his youthful vigour. Then he had tried to wake up Mags. The only trouble was that she wasn't just cold – she was dead, having succumbed in the night. This was the terrible truth of what his life was like now.

He had shouted for the guards to come, and to give them their due they had dragged the body away, but simply because they did not want corpses polluting the environment where the live workers were kept. Helmuth had snarled and made for their captives, and had been smacked down by the butt of a rifle, ending up with a bloodied head for his trouble.

After that Ben had been made to walk back into

the settlement of Valensis to collect the stones that were needed to complete the walls. The fortress was nearly done, and it was clear that another half day of labour would complete the task.

The horse and cart were further out than before. Valensis was not a large village by any means, and they had ended up on the boundaries on the far side of the bend, about as far from the fort as they were able to get and still collect materials.

He was with two of the women, obviously ones their captors thought suitable for such a menial task, and they were being supervised by a young man who was armed with an old Winchester that looked liked one of the originals from the early seventies. The youth had a fierce look about him that showed he would brook no argument from any of them, and his only conversation with them was an occasional sharp command to 'hurry, gringos'.

Ben thought of his father. His hopes, which had once been so bright, were fading fast as he looked down the barrel of a rifle that could end his life in a bare second. He would have given anything to hear his father's voice, or to see him again.

That was when the miracle happened. From the ruins of what had once been a dwelling place a shadowy figure appeared, rearing up behind the youth who was guarding the prisoners. Ben knew at once that the lack of food and his exhaustion must have caught up with him, that what he had hoped for was coming true. Yet he did not react, did not say anything, and the two women, who had been bending over to pick up more stones, hadn't seen anything at all.

The best of it was, the cart was being loaded from behind, while the so-called soldier stood and guarded them, so it was obscuring the view of anyone who might look over from one of the other work parties, who were doing the same kind of task.

There was a dull 'thunk' as a rock was smacked into the guard's head, and the youth fell to the ground. It was a sound that could just as easily have been made by one of the stones landing in the cart, and not even as loud.

Ben did not hesitate, he ran forward, about to give forth a cry of joyful surprise at this apparition of his father who had rescued him, but the figure put a finger to his lips. Typically Ben wanted the two women to come with him, but they only drew their skirts back and looked frightened at what had happened. And who could blame them? Their captors had shown that they were not particularly merciful, and anyone who attacked them would get short shrift indeed.

Now, as they ran together to the woodlands beyond the village Ben experienced a surge of joy that he had not felt in what seemed like years.

'You did it, I knew you weren't dead, Dad,' he said.

'Just keep on moving, Son. There's enough of them around there to notice what's happened,' said King speaking in a low voice.

Their journey might have been uninterrupted if

it had not been for a piece of bad luck, the kind that seemed to have been pursuing them both in the last few days. King was heading for where he had left his mare. Once mounted they could get away a lot more quickly, when there was a rustle in the woodlands, and the thick bushes parted to reveal four Mexicans who were carrying two dead antelope strung on poles.

King did not hesitate. He was not going to let anything stop him now. His gun was already in his hand and he was ready to shoot them down if they got in his way, and from the startled way in which they threw down their prey and scrambled for their own weapons it was clear they had not been expecting to meet an armed man either.

Clearly what had happened was that the fort was fast running out of food, the one weakness when so many needed to be fed, so Valsquez had sent out a hunting party for fresh supplies.

King was about to fire on them when he heard a grating voice behind him:

'Put down the weapon, *señor.*'

Wide-eyed he turned and saw that the four carrying the deer were not the only ones in the hunting party. There was an older man, and he had snatched Ben and was holding a pistol to his head.

Hernandez had led the hunting party. Food was growing short and it was time to replenish the larder not just with rabbits, fish and other small game, but with a proper catch. The men could

95

barely be spared because this was a small-scale rebellion, but the work had to be done or there would be unrest among the men. Those captured from Purgatory did not matter, of course, since he and Valsquez had no use for them once the great work was done. He did not go any further in his thoughts because he encountered the renegade and the boy. One of his talents was his ability to react quickly to a new situation. Now he was standing there holding a gun to the boy's head. Ben squirmed in his grasp, but his captor had a firm hold of the boy, and it was clear that he did not intend to let him get away.

'So, my friend, you have come back to kidnap one of our workers?'

'I kidnap nobody, he was leaving with me, as is his right as a free American citizen,' said King, 'as is my right, too.'

'Throw down your guns,' said Hernandez coldly, 'or I will exercise my right as a commander to splatter his brains across this woodland.' The captor had the cold, expressionless eyes of a snake. King had encountered such men many times during his life, but he had always been equal to the situation – but now he was trapped. The very weapons that could free him were also the one factor that could end the life of his one remaining family member. With a look of smouldering hatred he threw his guns into the dirt and watched as one of the hunters grabbed his weapons and pocketed them.

'March,' said Hernandez. It was about half a mile to the fort, and King and his son were made to walk the whole way with his own weapons trained on him. Such was the cussedness of fate: just a few moments earlier or later and he would never have encountered this leader, a meeting that had led to their capture.

Hernandez did not waste any time when they got to the fort, but marched King and his son straight to Valsquez.

Besides the two barracks, capable of holding up to five hundred soldiers, in one of which the prisoners were kept overnight, the fort held an administrative block in front of the barracks' buildings. This was a pleasing little building made of red brick, and it was more or less intact, with a sloping roof of grey tiles and larger windows than the barracks buildings. It was clearly the place where all the important decisions had been made when this was the headquarters of a borders' force.

The door was made of dark wood, and there was a brass knocker made to look like a lion's head on the front, which Hernandez used in a brisk fashion. It was evident that the knocker was new, probably taken from some artisan in the village. A soldier appeared dressed in the grey clothing adopted by all Valsquez' men, he saluted the new arrival and stood aside to let him enter.

Valsquez was in the main part of the building in what must once have been the administrative area. He had somehow conspired to furnish what must have been an empty space – he even had a large desk made of polished beech wood, which had probably belonged to the mayor of Valensis. King immediately realized that he was in the presence of genuine power, a charismatic leader who could inspire people to do what he wanted, no matter how mad his plans might turn out to be. He had heard of people like this before, such as Santa Ana or Jesse James, who could inspire whole legends. King himself did not lack in leadership skills, and he knew what he was up against.

'He was caught trying to liberate the boy,' said Hernandez. 'I was going to shoot them in the head, but look at the man! He is fit, he is strong, and he has the bearing of a leader, and we know him well already.'

'Thank you, my lieutenant,' said Valsquez, getting up from his seat. Somehow he had contrived to get a stuffed leather chair, once more enjoying the trappings of power. Some poor labourers must have dragged that all the way up from the village, along with the desk. He came over to where the new arrival stood beside his son.

King was proud of the young man: Ben stood there beside his father, his face impassive, only his wide eyes and icy stare proclaiming his feelings of hatred for their captors. Neither of the captives showed a trace of fear, both knowing instinctively it was the worst thing to do with men of this type.

The result was unexpected. Valsquez gave a wide smile. It did not sit well on his thin features and made him look rather vulpine, but it was a smile, nonetheless.

'I would like you both to have a drink with me,' he had wine, too, a large carafe rather than a bottle, and several glasses, all sitting on his desk.

'Are you not going to execute them right away?' said Hernandez, a little aghast at the way the meeting had gone.

'Victor, where are your manners? This is a touching scene, it is a father and son reunited after a sad parting, and you are a little lacking in hospitality. You may have some wine too.'

'I'd rather not,' said Hernandez, 'I have the great work to supervise.'

'Then go, do your work, I will see you shortly.' Hernandez gave a grunt of surprise and annoyance, saluted his general – for this rag-tail army still considered itself to be a real force – and stalked out of the room.

'You must forgive Victor, he is rather into his histrionics,' said Valsquez. There was still a guard inside the door, and another two outside. In addition, the so-called 'general' had a pistol stuck into his waistband and a sword at his side. Looking at him as he handed them their wine, there was a faint contempt in the eyes of John King.

'Drink, my guests, drink,' said Valsquez taking a sip from his own leaden crystal glass. 'One of the spoils of war,' he said. The other two drank, Ben spluttering a little as he did so, but the red wine warmed their bodies, as was intended.

'I have provided an exception for you because you are a brave man,' said Valsquez. 'What is your name?'

'King, John King,' said his captive, who had little to gain by holding back the information, 'and this is my son, Ben.'

'You are a hero, John King. When we captured the people from your little town you turned your home into a little fort and defended yourself well. When the bomb fell, your son here sprang forth and shot like a little demon, and was soon captured, but you – well, I saw the building collapse on you and I thought you were dead, but you killed five of my men. Five of them – you were ferocious, *señor.*'

Sipping his glass of wine, King felt a sudden chill go through his bones at these words that were spoken in mild tones, barely above a whisper.

'The capture of your village was for a reason. It is for a purpose that is greater than any of us, the return to our rights to become a full nation again.'

'I don't understand,' said King, but his eyes bore into those of his captor. 'The only thing I do know is that the American government will not hear of this kind of sedition on their borders, that they will come down on you with a force that will make your petty defences look weak, and you will all die for a futile cause.'

'That may be so,' said Valsquez in an even milder voice. It was not the answer that King was expecting to hear. He jerked his head up and stared at the leader. 'There is a cause here you know nothing about. What did you know before you came to be on this land?'

'I knew that I was given the right to go forwards

and make my own way.'

'What was your way? Tearing precious metals from the land? You had the biggest, most solid house in that town, you had all the weapons. Were you a mine owner, taking your profits from the sweat of those around you?'

'No, I wasn't a mine owner,' King hesitated before saying his next words. 'I was a medic, a kind of doctor.'

'What is a "kind" of doctor?'

'I don't have a fancy piece of paper that you hang on the wall. I was in the army, in the field; I saved many a person's life, picked up the knowledge on the job. The miners, they paid me to do the same thing.'

'So you did profit from the blood and sweat of those around you? You see, John King, it is the way of all things. We are here for a reason, to take back what was ours already by right.'

'You're a bunch of kidnappers and cowards!' said Ben, so hotly it was almost comical.

Valquez lifted his chin and looked silently at the boy for a moment.

'The path of leadership is a hard one. I had a wife and children too, but my children were taken away from me by poverty and disease. Do you know what I am, both of you?'

'Do you really want me to say?' asked King.

'I am a rebel,' said Valsquez, 'a man who approached your government and spoke to them in peaceful terms and asked for our land to be given back to us. No, I don't mean the entire state of Texas, I am not that stupid, I mean these border-lands that constituted our ancestral lands.'

'But your people made agreements over the land, with their respective governments.'

'Not my people, not my representatives,' said Valsquez. 'I have lived all my life in the shadow of what was taken from my father, and the fathers of all the men who have joined me in our cause. We are the Abolitionists with a capital "A", and we will fight to take back what is ours.'

'But you have hardly any backing, by the looks of it,' said King reasonably. 'Do you really think this can end in anything but tears for all concerned?'

'You fool,' Valsquez walked over to where his prisoner stood, and slapped him across the face, hard. His small black pupils bore into those of his prisoner. His breath was sickly sweet from the wine. 'Nothing – that is what you know – nothing!'

CHAPTER FOURTEEN

Lucas sat with the group as they made their plans to fight the bandits, but there was a look on his face that said he was worried, and he approached the one man who could do anything about the matter. They walked a little away from the rest to converse in peace.

'Señor Carter, I saw the look on the face of your commander. He is not just leaving here to have some kind of think.'

'Lucas, do you know something, I think you're right,' said Carter. 'I guess I accepted what he was saying just because of whom he is, but there's often a case for arguing beyond a man's words.'

'Then we should take a look-see; bring the magic eyeglass that makes things close.'

'In this case I think you're right.' Carter did not want to cause disquiet by mentioning what his friend might be doing to the rest for a simple reason: the people here had already fled from a great deal of trouble; they might want to retreat again if they thought that the leader who might bring back their village had simply vanished.

'I'm going to go for another look' said Carter, 'see how much further they've got with their building work and assess the situation a little more. I guess we were scared they might spot us when we were all there, but Lucas is taking me back.' Nobody protested about this. Having a look at the strength of the enemy was a basic technique of war, except no one had used that word yet.

The two of them made their way back to the wooded vantage point from where they could observe the fort and the village beyond.

'Although he couldn't be sure because of the distance, John thought he saw Ben working at loading stone,' said Carter. 'Let's have a look.' He had borrowed the spyglass and surveyed the land beyond the fort. It took a while to focus, but he saw a large man and a smaller figure assiduously loading an old cart. He had known the boy well, but it was hard to tell at this distance.

'Maybe we were wrong,' he said to Lucas, 'I guess John's a bit more sensible than I thought he was. Not a man to let his feelings dictate what he's going to do.'

'Can I look?' Lucas took the spyglass and in his excitement put the wrong end to his right eye, 'this is too small!' Then realized his mistake and turned it round and looked through it correctly. 'No!' he cried, it seemed that he was looking at an opportune moment.

'Let me see,' Carter wrested the glass from the boy and took another look. He was just in time to see a changed scene. The guard was lying prone on the ground and the boy had vanished. The big man was still there looking around in a bewildered fashion, but it wasn't long before he, too, ran off into the woodlands surrounding the village.

'The fool, the bloody fool,' said Carter. 'I should have known – that boy, he's all that's left of his family.'

'Let's get out of here and tell the others. We can celebrate when Mister King comes back with his boy,' said Lucas joyfully, although still keeping his voice low.

'Not yet,' said Carter, 'I want to make sure that he got away. Besides, we can take a look at the fortifications again.' He trained the glass on the fort. It seemed that the walls were close to completion – another half day and they would be finished. A wave of despair flooded over him. When he had decided to turn back and help his friend, and had cajoled the other two into coming with him, things had seemed so simple. Once they were armed they would find a way of fighting the rebels and get the boy back. Imagination was so basic like that, while real life was a great deal more complex.

'Look,' said Lucas, 'people come back.' He did not have the spyglass, but he had the sharp eyes of youth and had seen the tiny figures in the distance.

Carter trained the spyglass on the figures pointed out by his companion and gave a groan of despair.

'They've got him,' he said, 'I thought he would get away, I thought John could do anything. Our leader's gone, it's the end.'

He sat there for what seemed like an age to his young companion, then put away the spyglass, a grim look on his face.

'Well, that's done,' he said, 'let's get out of here.'

Valsquez pulled away from the prisoners and sat down heavily behind his desk. It was obvious that he had taken more of the wine than was good for him.

'I am sorry for giving way to anger,' he said, 'a true ruler would rise above all that, and that is what I must do. You do not understand what is involved here. I have the backing of three states in my native country: Tamaulipas, Coahuila and Chihuahua, and many there are waiting to see what I will do. I have been promised much in the way of men and money when I show what can be created by rallying our people over here.'

'I have heard of this kind of thing before,' said King coldly. 'You have captured a wild border area that was once crucial in the civil war when our country was fighting on two fronts. You are hoping to stir nationalist fever and raise enough rebel hordes to overwhelm the border between your country and Texas.'

'You are wrong, King,' said Valquez. Now there was an air of triumph in his voice, 'I don't intend to

106

restore this border with my country, but *all* of them.'

This was a staggering thought. Valsquez spoke with such conviction that for a moment King almost believed in what he was saying, that the man had enough vision to achieve his aim, such was the force of his personality.

'I don't want to argue with you,' said King, 'but you are talking about thousands of miles here, so why do you think one little rebellion here would achieve that result?'

'You don't understand either, my prisoner,' said Valsquez. 'I am here to foment a rebellion amongst those who live on the borders. It is a time of economic unrest in your country, and once those of my people who live there see what can be done, this will cause trouble for those thousands of miles. Have you ever seen a row of dominoes set up so that they are behind one another in a long line?'

'That's what I used to do,' said Ben, the picture of what it had been like in his head.

'I see, my boy – and what happens when you flick those dominoes with your finger?'

'They hit each other and they all fall down.'

'You see?' It was a good analogy, because they could immediately see what he was getting at without any further explanation.

'I hate to put a dampener on your little scheme,' said King, 'but the Texas rangers will put paid to your fort long before that happens.'

'You have never been more wrong,' said Valsquez

107

seriously. 'The Texas rangers are a spent force, such forces cost money, and at this time the funds are not there. Once we repel one force, the word will get out and the battle will draw even more rebels to our cause.'

It was clear that he was getting near to the end of his conversation with them. His face was flushed and there was a weary look about him.

'I just don't understand why you had to go to the lengths of taking our people like you did. You had already captured the village.'

'We made our plans – myself and Victor Hernandez – a few months ago when we were getting the finance for what we were doing. We had a setback in that there was disease in the village. We learned of the disease, known as 'the black dog' to our people, and held back so that it would end in a natural way. But we couldn't wait too long, so as soon as we learned the disease had run its course, we came in.'

'I see what you were doing,' said King. 'You didn't recruit your men here purely through loyalty, you paid them to be here, didn't you? The average peon probably earns tiny wages in the fields, so you offered them a great deal more, didn't you? This is really a mercenary army.'

'And what army is not, my friend? You are wrong though, my men fight for a just cause.' It was clear that the leader was going to get to the point of making them leave.

'But you were telling me about the village.'

'Ah, that is an example of how a great leader rises to the occasion. We had calculated that when we took over there would be more than enough of our people to restore Fort Geffen, as it was then called. It shall now be known as Fort Freedom, and it will be a rallying point for all of our kind. The trouble was that many of the older and younger ones had died, and we were not certain who had the disease any more. When we began to recruit we had to hold back and take only the healthy ones while the others fled, and my men, afraid of the disease, let them go.'

King could picture the scene. Plans that had been made to restore a symbol of freedom had been broken because of one of nature's more unpleasant events, the spread of an infectious illness.

'That was when Victor remembered the land once owned by his not-so-distant ancestors, and the fact that it was populated by those who mined the earth, hardy workers who could serve our cause if they were brought here.'

'You must be proud,' said King. 'You brought down two communities, needlessly destroying them for your cause.'

'I tire of this,' said Valsquez, and indeed the flush that had appeared on his cheeks, along with the twin hollows that were his eyes, showed that he was a man on the verge of exhaustion. 'I thought it would be good to talk as one leader to another, to show why a man has to stand up for his people.'

'For self glory,' said King, who should have held himself back, but couldn't help stating what was on his mind.

'Enough,' Valsquez held up a weary hand. 'Guards, come here, take away these two. Separate them and get them to work on the great glory of restoration. It is all right, they do not have the disease.' Two of the so-called soldiers came forward, grabbed them and took them away from their commander.

Hernandez was waiting for them outside. When he heard from the guards what had been said, he gave a smile that was not in the least humorous.

'Get the boy back to fetching stones. But the man – set him up high, finishing the final work with the rest. Then we will see how many mouths we have to feed.'

'Father!' said Ben as he was dragged away.

'Don't worry, Son, this will end soon, and we'll win,' said King. He gave a groan and fell to his knees as Hernandez hit him hard between the shoulder blades.

'Get out there and do the only kind of work you are fit for. The glorious end is nearly here! You will pay for what your kind has done.'

King found himself put in with those he had last been with; he was greeted with stares of recognition, but under armed guard, those ragged, cowed people did not dare speak. One or two of the people of Valensis were there too, but he noticed the guards remained aloof from them, probably still fearing the spread of the disease but still needing workers. King was set to work climbing a tall wooden ladder, with stone in a sling on his back, like an obscene baby. The walls were nearly done, and he knew as he handed up the stone to be put in place by one of the builders that soon it would be the end, then all the prisoners would die. He had tried to rescue his son for nothing.

CHAPTER FIFTEEN

Hernandez sat with his commander, looking at him with an enigmatic expression.

'I have come to talk with you about the new prisoner, my leader.'

'I have spoken with him,' said Valsquez. 'You have made him part of the great work?'

'Did you notice something about him?'

'I saw a man who was a leader in his own community. I wanted to examine him as a curiosity, no more. It is not often you get to kill a man and then get to meet him again.'

'Did you not observe the look of the man? He was clean and well fed and well rested. What does that say to you?'

'It tells me that here is a man who has made plans to do what has to be done.'

'I say it is worse than that. He has clearly been elsewhere. His son has been here for days, yet he never appeared. That means he has been making preparation somewhere else, and the way he knew where to get the boy. It argues to me that he was spying on us.'

'I think so too,' said Valsquez. 'But we are nearly finished here, it hardly matters what he has been doing.'

'I disagree,' said Hernandez. 'The way he looked around and knew what to do, I think he has been led here by some of the reprobates who escaped, that somehow he encountered them.'

'I do not see your argument. We are practically impregnable here.'

'My leader, I think you need to rest and consider matters. No fort is impregnable, even with strong new walls.'

'You are right,' Valsquez gave a heavy sigh. 'This was not a man who was cowed by what happened to him, terrible though it was. He came to rescue his son on an impulse.'

'It is an impulse that will cost him dear,' said Hernandez grimly. 'I would ask you for permission to get information from him.' The smile he gave when he said this would have made a small child scream. 'I made a small error, I sent the boy back out to work, to gather the last few stones with others, less than an hour ago, but it is the work of five minutes to get him back.'

'Very well,' said Valsquez, 'and do it the right way – use the boy as a lever to get his co-operation.'

'My very thought,' said Hernandez as he strode out of the building.

*

113

Ben was happy to be out of the fort and back down at the village loading rocks along with Helmuth. The young guard, Miguel, who was supervising the loading of the cart, kept them inside the boundaries of the village and looked around nervously as he did so. He was, like most of the recruits, about twenty years of age. He had the arrogance of youth and the certainty that what he was doing was right, but there was a certain lack of experience about him.

Ben suddenly found that he was imbued with a new spirit. The discovery that his father was still alive had renewed his hopes that he would escape from this fresh hell. He turned to Miguel and taunted the young man.

'You're all going to die, you know that, don't you?'

'Shut up,' said Miguel, training a rifle on the boy.

'That's real smart,' said Ben, 'kill me and you'll have to load this thing yourself.' Miguel relaxed a little and lowered his rifle.

This, of course, was the moment to strike, and Ben was holding one of the smaller rocks especially for that purpose. Thinking too much is fatal in these conditions, and he didn't stop to consider what he was doing, but simply threw the rock as hard as he could. It caught the young man full on the chest and must have cracked a couple of ribs straight away. Miguel doubled over in pain, and Ben scrabbled forwards, snatched his rifle and pulled it out of his nerveless hands.

114

Without thinking too much again, Ben ran towards the forest beside the village. Helmuth ran in the opposite direction, down a side road that would take him to the river where he could dive in and swim for safety.

As the boy ran there was the crack of a rifle shot and some dust kicked up beside him. He began weaving as he ran and this saved his life because the dirt kicked up again just where he had been a few seconds before. He ran into the trees and turned briefly just in time to see that a burly guard was running after him. Ben turned and fired and the guard fell to the ground cursing and clutching at his right leg. The village had been largely empty because that part of the job was nearly finished, and no one else chased after him at that precise second.

Ben didn't wait. This was his second escape on the same day, and he was under no illusions about what would happen to him if he was caught. He would be killed this time as a troublemaker who was getting in the way of the great cause.

The one problem he had was that he didn't know where to go. He was on his own, and he was lost. Running through the trees he knew that he could not stay here for long. Some of the people who were taking part in the rebellion were from this district, and they would be able to track him down.

Then a deep voice spoke in a calm but urgent tone from amongst the trees.

'Come with me, I'll help you.'

He stopped, raising the rifle at the same time and

115

looked in that direction. A big man dressed like a trail rider, who looked all too familiar, was beckoning to him. Gratefully Ben followed. He was being rescued.

King came down the ladder and found that Hernandez was waiting for him. The second-in-command had a peculiar expression on his face, a mixture of joy and intolerant anger that showed his captive that he had some intent to find out more. King himself had been thinking while he was carrying out the physical labour. He knew that his men were still at liberty, and he knew he could count on them to try and rescue him, although he did not know precisely what they were going to do. And although they had parted him from Ben, they had set the boy back to work, which meant he was away from the capricious leaders of the rebellion.

'Come with me,' said Hernandez, undoing all of this in a single stroke. King followed, not because he wanted to, but because the second-in-command had two armed guards with him who looked quite capable of using their firepower if he disobeyed.

He was led to a building beside the main administration block. It was a grim, granite-looking structure that betrayed its origins at a glance.

'This was the prison block,' he said, 'and not just for captives, for anyone who did not obey commands.' He led the prisoner inside. The building had a smell of dampness and decay. Some box-like cells lined one of the walls, their iron bars rusted, some of them distinctly damaged showing that the former occupants had not taken things lying down. Hernandez took his prisoner into a big, mildew-stained room, with bare walls. There was a large wooden chair in the room, the only new object there.

'Tie him to the chair,' said Hernandez, a grim smile on his face. The soldier obeyed, using lengths of old rope that had been especially prepared for that purpose.

'You will know why I am here,' said Hernandez.

'I don't know anything,' said King, 'just that you and your people are breaking the law of the land at every turn.'

'Silence!' the big man took off his tunic and his hat, and handed them to his subordinate. For someone who was an aristocrat in his own land, he was well muscled. King guessed that he must been a sportsman in his youth. 'You will answer the questions I ask. You will tell me the truth, then you can go back to work with the rest.'

'What do you want to know, Hernie?' asked King, determined not to be cowed. Hernandez slapped him across the face, hard.

'And none of that insolent talk, my friend. You and your type are the reason why we are here. Now, how did you get here?'

'On a horse,' said King. Hernandez slapped him again and King could feel his face throbbing with the heat of the blow.

'This is how it works. You tell me the truth, I

117

listen. You talk back, I hit you. How does that sound?' King remained silent. 'Good, then you will answer my question, my good friend.'

'When your leader murdered my family I decided it was time to fight back.' King did not mention Ben, and he was hoping that this was a weakness that his interrogator would not spot. 'But the problem was, I was nearly dead myself. I took a few days to recover and that's why I came along so late.'

'So who is with you?'

'No one, I came here on my own.' King knew that the walls were as good as finished, and that meant that Valsquez would have plenty of men whom he could deploy elsewhere, such as using them to hunt down the refugees from the village below. If King betrayed them the hunt would take up much less time. He decided that this was not something he wanted on his conscience. He used the same strength of character that had allowed him to exist in Purgatory for years without falling victim to their ways.

'Are you sure, Señor?' asked Hernandez in a mock friendly fashion.

'I don't need to hold hands with anyone else, like some pantywaist,' said King, pretending to be angry at the implication that he was weak enough to need others. The anger was real enough, though, because he used the angst at his current imprisonment to fuel his rage.

'I think you are lying,' said Hernandez. He stepped back and put a hand to his chin and looked

118

thoughtful. 'And I will tell you what: I know that many fled from here, and I think that you know where they are. People of our own kind could be useful for the cause. I think you are a strong man and that you would take a lot of pain for a cause, but would you take it for your son?'

'You keep my son out of this.' King knew that his bluff had been called. He might have had the fortitude to deal with this situation on his own, but there was no way he could let his son suffer. Hernandez sensed that he had the upper hand, and spoke in a soft, almost hypnotic voice.

'I will let you be reunited with your son if you just tell me what I want to know, otherwise you will both suffer terribly, and he is young. I don't know if he could stand much of this.' And Hernadez punched King in the chest with such force that for a few moments his prisoner had to fight to get his breath.

'Bastard,' said King.

There was the sound of shuffling feet from outside and a voice raised in protest: 'No, I must see him.'

Hernandez looked annoyed, but he also knew that in these circumstances he must respond to every event. It was obvious that one of the soldiers wanted to contact his leader. He looked at King with a jaundiced eye.

'Wait where you are, as if you have any choice,' and marched out of the room. The prison block was not exactly soundproof, and King strained his ears to hear what had happened.

119

'The boy, he is gone,' the words were said in an excited babble, in Spanish. Miguel had recovered enough to tell his commander. No one could live in this part of the world without picking up a smattering of the language, and with having to deal with so many people King had picked up more than most.

'Get outside,' said Hernandez immediately, and the man was taken away, still babbling. There was a pause as the muted sounds continued, and King was no longer able to hear what was being said. Then there was the sharp crack of a gunshot and the sound of excited voices, and King knew that what had happened was a classic case of shooting the messenger. King heard the scuffing of leather boots on the hard ground, and then the sound of Hernandez' heavy body coming back to the old prison, and he smiled through his pain. He didn't know where his son was, but for the moment at least Ben was safe, and his enemy had no bargaining tool.

CHAPTER SIXTEEN

Those who had fled the regime of the Abolitionists surrounded the travellers who were left. Carter had departed, grim-faced, on an errand of his own, despite Vetters and Sutton trying to restrain him. He had muttered about 'doing something', but had promised to come back as soon as he was finished. There was a wild look in his eyes that Vetters didn't like; it was one of the reasons that Carter was considered a lone wolf back in the mining community, where he held himself aloof from much of the roistering that went on and concentrated on his business – getting precious metals from the ground. He was an intense man who shared little, but could be depended on in a time of need.

Quinto, Juan and Riaz were brought into the discussion because, of all the people in the twenty or so from the fort town, they were the ones who had the greatest desire to fight back against the forces who had taken their world from them. Living out here in makeshift shelters wasn't easy. The nights were cold, and most were suffering because they had very little in the way of warm coverings. Even the tents were leftovers from other expeditions to the wild. It was Vetters who spoke to them in a forthright manner.

'My father was a soldier, and I like to think I've got some of his better qualities. He was stationed here in this old fort.' Vetters took a deep breath and seemed to consider the matter deeply. 'He didn't like to talk about some of the things that happened here, the border wars he fought in, the Civil War, but he did talk about the fort. If I'm right, and you can tell me if my memory is faulty here, do any of you know, was there ever a talk of a way into the fort that wasn't through the gates?'

Quinto and his companions shook their heads.

'I was never told of such a thing,' said Quinto. 'I just remember when I was a young child that bits of the walls were still being used to build up our town.'

Juan and Riaz agreed with their leader. In despair Vetters looked at the other twenty or so assembled people.

'Have any of you heard anything like this? Look, I'll tell you what was said. The Brazos has many tributaries in this area, and my father said that the fort was built on one of those outflows. He said it was done deliberately because the downfall of many forts is that when they are under siege they are unable to get supplies. Besides, this "back door", if

you want to call it such, was a way of troops getting
out in ones and twos and having a stab at killing the
enemy before retreating again.'

'I remember that,' said Sutton with a sudden
smile, 'they called them "ghost soldiers", didn't
they, when they appeared and took sniper shots at
the surrounding enemy?'

'That's right,' said Vetters. 'Has anybody heard
anything about this?'

'Nothing,' said Alice, 'my grandfather fought in
the war, but he never mentioned that phrase.' She
looked at Lucas, who was hanging his head and
looking at the ground. 'Lucas, what's wrong?'

'I got dirt in my eye,' said the young man as he
lifted his head. He was saying this to save face, as the
grime on his features was faintly streaked with tears.
Vetters was quick to pick up on what was happening.

'You've heard of what I'm talking about?'

'Yes, I have, *señor*. I used to come out here with
my friends and my cousins, who are also friends. We
have a way of life called the "wild time", where our
parents know we are young and filled with the devil.
That is when we go into the wild and hunt and
shoot and fish and explore like all young people
must do.'

'That's good,' said Vetters. 'But it doesn't solve
any puzzles right here and now.'

'I once got taken away from my friends,' said
Lucas. 'They thought they had spotted the tracks of
a bear, and I was younger and couldn't keep up with

them. The truth is, I was lost in this wild land, because in their excitement they left me behind. I decided to wait where I was beside one of the many streams until they came back – and then I noticed the stream seemed to go into the rock face. I followed that water, and soon found that there was a break in the wall big enough for me to stand up in. I began to follow it along, and I soon found the water was going through, but there was a way up the rock, but this time inside the cliff. It was dark in there, and I was much afraid, so I went back out and I found my friends and we went away. They never did find that bear.'

'Wait a minute,' said Sutton. 'Are you saying that that could be the way into the fort? But there's countless cracks in the cliff face around this area, I saw many of them when we were unwittingly on our way here – so couldn't it be that you had just found another passage made that way over the years by the natural rise and fall of the land?'

'*Señor*, yes, that could be the way of it,' said Lucas, with such a look of relief on his face that they were all fooled for a moment – except for Alice. She bent down on one knee beside him and put a hand on his shoulder and looked into his face.

'That's not all, is it?'

'No, *señorita*, but I can't say.' Then Lucas thought for a moment longer, and straightened up as one who has made a decision. 'In fact, the truth is, I went back. I had a torch made out of wood with pitch to make it burn well, and I went up inside the passage.'

'And?' pressed the girl.

'It is like you already know: it goes up inside the fort, at the back of the barracks where the ground is earthy.'

'You'll lead us there, won't you Lucas?' asked the girl.

'The soldiers, they'll kill us all,' he said in a voice that rose barely above a whisper.

His cousins looked at him, their faces fierce, but Quinto had a tone of understanding in his voice.

'Cousin, if you lead us there, that is all that matters – believe us when we say we will do the rest. You will be safe.'

'But then if I do not fight I will be called a coward for ever,' said Lucas. Vetters came over with Sutton and they looked at him.

'Hell, we ain't blaming you,' said Sutton. 'But this is too big for us to leave alone. Believe you me, if you help us out with this, no one will ever call you anything or they'll have me to answer to.' The youth brightened up at these words.

'And as for you, young lady,' said Vetters, 'you used the word "we" when you was talking about this here expedition. But you'll stay right here with the rest of the women folks.'

Alice stood up slowly and wiped her hands together. She was a tall woman and came up to his chin.

'This is my fight as much as it's yours. That man saved my life for sure, and he risked everything for his son.' Before they could argue further there was a shout from the person guarding the pass.

'It's Señor Carter – and he's brought someone with him.'

CHAPTER SEVENTEEN

The walls had their first test within hours of the fort being finished. The prisoners were herded away in the barracks and only a few guards were manning the ramparts when the sky broiled with black clouds and the rain began to fall. Hernandez came out from the prison block where he had been interrogating his prisoner at the first shout from one of his men. He did not have to go for his leader, who came out of the administrative quarters of his own volition. The two men stood there as the wind rose to a screaming howl, and simply waited.

This was the moment when they would know if their dreams would turn to dust or not. The mortar had dried out swiftly, but this was a test to see if it held.

The storm went on for several hours and the ground was awash with water – but the designers of the fort had even thought of that circumstance, and there were holes in the ground at intervals covered by iron grates where the water drained away. The two leaders were not there for long, and both returned to their respective tasks.

At last the rain petered out and the winds died down, and the sunshine came back as the clouds rolled away. The walls were as high as ever.

Valsquez was inspecting the fort. The prisoners had all been herded back into one of the old barrack rooms and the doors had been bolted on them. The soldiers had been unsparing in their efforts to get them away so that their revered leader could inspect the work that had been done. Valsquez came out of the administrative block dressed in his blue and gold uniform and wearing his splendid tri-cornered hat. He was accompanied by Hernandez, and the first thing he did when he emerged was to look at the soldiers who were assembled at the newly built ramparts. He saluted them gravely and they responded in kind. When assembled they did not add up to a huge number of men, totalling about twenty in all, not counting those who were still out hunting game, who numbered another eight. He had started off with many more men. Some had fallen by the wayside, some had deserted, and some had been killed in Purgatory; the remainder were his loyal servants.

Starting at the furthest corner where the repairs had been done, he walked slowly along the newly repaired walls, crossed over the cobbled path at the heavily barred entrance to the fort, and inspected the second wall as gravely as he had the first.

After this was done he stepped back to his own quarters, standing well back so that he could see his assembled troops.

'My comrades, you have done a great thing. Your efforts are a huge step towards us getting back what has been taken from us by force and political strategy. You are disabling the enemies of our people, and your names will go down in glorious history for what you have done!' He smiled at them, allowing the stern expression to drop for a moment and saluted them again. They cheered in unison and he waved his arms at them.

'You may relax and drink. There is alcohol from the village, but I warn you just for today, you will always be on duty, for this is just the beginning.' He saluted them again as they cheered loud and long, then he turned and went back inside the administrative block.

Once he was inside his quarters, with only Hernandez accompanying him, he stumbled forwards and found his seat, removing his hat, which he set down beside him, and pushed a hand through his treacle-black hair. Droplets of sweat could be seen on his forehead, and the hand that went through his locks was trembling.

'You are ill, Jorge,' said Hernandez in a low voice so that the guards outside the door could not hear.

'I have a fever, that is all,' said the leader dismissively. 'Did you see that out there, what they have achieved?'

'It is a fine piece of work,' said Hernandez dryly. 'I did not think it possible in some ways. Are you sure you will be fit for the fight, for as you say, this is the beginning, not the end?'

'I will rest for a few hours,' said Valsquez, 'then it will be time for the next part of the plan – to spread the insurrection amongst our people.'

'The rewards will be great,' said Hernandez. 'I will get back my lands, and I am sure as your loyal servant I will be given more on top of that. I hope so, because that gorge that once contained gold has been worked out, it will no longer yield a profit, the Americans have sucked it dry. But with the rich lands around here I could raise cattle and sheep and make huge profits.'

'What are you saying?' Valsquez started up, his cheeks blazing, and not just with the fever. 'Do you think I do this for money? I started this revolution for my people, so that they can come out of what is no more than serfdom.'

'The point is not the money,' said Hernandez, 'it is the power that we will have in this land, and when it is seen what we have done, thousands will rally to our cause. You are our symbol, our glorious leader.'

They both knew this was true, that a cause needed a leader whom others could look up to, and Valsquez was that leader. He had been spreading the word in the borderlands for many years, making legal challenges to the American government one after the other. Without such a leader a cause could appear too nebulous, too scattergun, but a leader with a simple wish – to take back lands annexed in an unfair and unequal treaty – would get his share of the disgruntled and disaffected, many of whom would regard themselves as cheated by a settlement, even one that was legal on both sides.

'The revolution begins,' said Hernandez, 'and that is the important point. Now,' he moved on to a more immediately pressing point, 'what are we going to do with King?'

'I don't think we can do much,' said Valsquez, 'except to make him an object lesson. Have him tied up in the middle of the marching square, and let all see what he has become, a leader brought to nothing. You will see, it will keep them cowed.'

'Why do we bother keeping them alive at all?' asked Hernandez. 'Now the work is done, why don't we just finish them off and have done with it? The woods are dark and deep and hide plenty of sins.'

'That is the point, Victor: these are not just our slaves, and they are citizens of America. It is our duty to keep them alive – unless they rebel and we have to shoot some of them – because they are our ultimate bargaining counter. You spoke about power? Well, they are our power against forces who might try to bring us down.' He did not use the words, but they both knew he was talking about the Texas Rangers.

'They need only a few scraps of meat and some vegetables, and they will live. So do what you must, but make this King an example of what will happen

131

if they resist. If they rose all at once they could overcome us, you know – a few of them might be killed,
but our troops are so few that they would be over-
whelmed by sheer numbers.'

'Very well, I will let you rest.' Hernandez saluted his
general and walked out of the building. He went into
the prison block. King was in one of the cells. He
looked distinctly the worse for wear, having been
questioned thoroughly, and beaten severely in the
process, but despite severe bruising about the face,
neck and body, he maintained that he was on his own.

And Hernandez, who had done much of the
interrogation, believed him. Besides, the fort was
finished now and it was invulnerable, and there was
little that King's companions – if they did exist –
could do.

'Time for you to be an example,' said
Hernandez. There was a large courtyard in front of
the barracks, with a well situated to the left-hand
side surrounded by a low wall, and on the other side
of the square was a thick wooden post set into the
ground. This was where soldiers had been whipped
for insubordination. King was brought out and tied
to this by ropes at his wrists, waist and ankles.

He was physically weak because the beatings had
taken their toll, but his face was as impassive as ever.

'The night rolls on,' said Hernandez. 'You will be
here until dawn, and if you are still alive you will go
in with the others. If not, you will lie on the rocks
and have your bones picked clean by the vultures.'

King said nothing. He was not in a good condition,

and the chances were that as the night rolled on and the temperature dropped he would die where he stood.

Hernandez wasted no more time. He had his troops lead out the builders of the walls, the people of Purgatory, and he showed them their former leader. The people shuffled by, men and women, all cowed by sheer physical exhaustion and the guns trained on him.

'This is what you will get if you defy your orders. This man thought he could usurp our command, and the same will happen to you all if you rebel.' The villager's shuffled on, barely able to look him in the face, but King lifted his head and watched them move, saying nothing.

'Our glorious leader has ordered blankets and bedding to be brought for you,' said Hernandez to the villagers. 'You will be fed and treated well. Now retreat and ponder on these matters,' and the villagers were herded back into the barracks.

King's head drooped again. Hernandez came over and grabbed King's overlong hair and pulled his head up so they were face to face.

'Die or live, we win.'

King spat in his face. Furious, Hernadez punched him in the solar plexus, and King gasped and shuddered and would have fallen if it had not been for the ropes.

Hernandez wiped away the spittle with a spotted bandanna and walked off, with no more to say. And the night wore on.

133

CHAPTER EIGHTEEN

Jos Carter took over the command with his men. This seemed to be his moment, for he had carried out a daring act that even King had not been able to do; the fact that he just happened to be in the right time and place had little to do with the matter – the return of Ben was a symbol of hope. They had gathered together on the same evening that King was being interrogated, and watched in silence under the shelter of the trees and rocky overhangs as the rain poured down, sheets of water from heaven.

If the rain continued it would mean they would have to postpone their raid for another day – but as Carter pointed out to them, this could be fatal, for more of Valsquez' supporters could appear in that time and swell their numbers. Fortunately the rain stopped, and although more of the same might be threatening from the east, it kept off long enough for them to continue.

'We'll arm all the able-bodied men,' he said briskly.

'I'm coming too,' said Ben.

'Me too,' said Lucas.

Their new leader did not demur at this. Lucas was essential to them as a guide, at least in the beginning, and Ben had earned the right to help in the rescue of his father. As for Quinto, Riaz and Juan, they were absolutely essential since they were young and lithe and hated Valsquez more than anyone else there for what he had done to their homes.

'We'll go at first light,' said Carter. 'You will lead the way Lucas, taking us to the correct place.'

'I'm going to be there as well,' said Alice.

'I'm afraid that ain't happening,' said Carter, and the girl said nothing – but there was a look on her face that said the matter was not going to rest there.

Ben was invaluable. He had actually helped to rebuild the fort, and he had seen the restored doors and walls. Lucas was helpful, too – he had played in the fort with his friends when they were young, and he had a good memory for where the entrances to the barracks and the other buildings were.

Together they were able to scratch out a layout on the ground that showed where everything was, including the quarters where Valsquez would be housed. Quinto and his friends examined this closely, and along with Carter, Vetters and Sutter committed the layout to memory. It was all very well being able to get inside the fort, but quite another to know where everything was. Another ten of the villagers were coming too, and they would be behind the main force, ready to take on the invaders.

Carter stood up. He had been poring over the plans, but now the light was starting to fade. He had been a miner for many years, and the thought of going underground didn't bother him in the least, but he was clever enough to know this was not the case for everybody.

'Tomorrow we are going to defeat evil. We have all been affected by this in one way or another. We are going to check our weapons now. I don't have enough guns to arm everybody, but we have clubs and knives we can use. The first thing we will do is release our people, and then we will fight until the end. Just now we'll go and get a good night's rest, for we will need to be alert and ready for what is to be done.'

It said a lot for the trust that had built up amongst them that he armed the three young men without a moment of hesitation. This wasn't a war between people of different types, it was a war between those who wanted to take back the border-lands and those who wanted to remain in what had become their homeland.

Alice said nothing as the men were armed. She already had the knife that she had brought with her. She slept in a tent with three of the women from Valensis; the quarters were cramped, but it did mean that they could huddle together for warmth against the cold and damp of the night. It took her a long time to fall asleep because of the thoughts that went through her mind: she too wanted to play her part, and no one was going to stop her.

It was barely dawn when Valsquez and Hernandez appeared from their quarters and walked slowly across the square to the man who was tied to the stake. The air was cold around their shoulders. Hernandez was in robust good health, but Valsquez did not look well. The fever that had been taking hold of him was rising and his cheeks were an unhealthy red. Hernandez had wanted to go on his own, but the leader had insisted on coming with him.

Tied to the stake as he was, his head dropping down to his chin, his body still, it looked as if King had succumbed to the beatings and the cold of the night.

'Fetch me a bucket of water,' said Valsquez to one of the two soldiers who were still on duty. There had been many celebrations the night before, and these ones had taken over their watch with barely enough sleep, having consumed a good amount of alcohol the night before. The soldier saluted and went to the well. There was a wooden bucket on a rope beside the well and he dropped the bucket down while holding on to the rope. He hesitated a moment before pulling the bucket back up.

'What's wrong, man?' asked Hernandez testily.

'It seems to be caught sir,' said the soldier. 'Ah no, here it is.' He drew the bucket back up, carried it over to his leaders and set it down before them.

'First, I am thirsty,' said Valsquez. He took out a silver cup from his breast pocket that he often filled with red wine to refresh himself on long journeys. Also, because it was his own personal cup there was less chance of being poisoned, which was another of the reasons why he brought it with him.

He took several draughts of the clear liquid and looked visibly better, the flush on his face subsiding somewhat; then he picked up the bucket and threw the rest of the water over King.

The effect was electrifying: King gave a gasp as he drew in a sharp breath and lifted his head whilst straining his body against the ropes.

'You bastards,' he said. 'Rot in hell!'

'You are a brave man,' said Valsquez. 'I never thought you would survive, but as your reward you will go to the others and be part of them until our colony is established and our glorious revolution begins.'

'You'll all die like the rats you are,' said King, but his teeth were chattering and it was obvious that he was suffering from the cold. The two guards were summoned and cut him down. King fell to his knees on the cobbled ground, and the two guards jerked him to his feet and half carried, half dragged him to the barracks where the prisoners were kept. They unbarred the door and threw him inside.

'A brave man, but a foolish one to act alone as he did,' said Valsquez. His companion had already told him about the poor results of the interrogation, and the leader had come to believe that King really had been acting on his own.

'You need to rest now,' said Hernandez in a solic-itous manner, and he returned with his leader to their quarters, leaving the soldiers guarding an empty courtyard.

CHAPTER NINETEEN

The dawn was there, but the make-do troops were ready long before the first light, seeing their way by low fires. They were armed with a mixture of guns and rifles and they had all been briefed in what they were to do. The numbers were small – some fifteen in all who had been deemed fit to carry out their task and Carter was, by some kind of unacknowledged vote, cast in the role of leader. He was not the kind of man who thought he had this quality in him, being a natural lone wolf, but there was a calm authority on him, along with his ability to reason in a logical manner, that had put him in the role.

One other quality about Carter stood out and attracted the others to him, and that was his unswerving loyalty to his friend John King. Their former leader might have been taken by the men in the fort, but Carter was not about to abandon their plans because of this problem: his friendship was absolute.

The air was still cold and the men were shivering a little as they were led out of the camp towards the pass that led to the outside world. There was a kind of crisp, fresh smell in the air in contrast to the dank scent of where they had been hiding, and the men unconsciously braced their bodies for what was to come. And as they made their way along, most of them wearing dark clothes, they blended into the background of rocks and trees and became nearly invisible. No wonder the Indians had called the men from the fort 'Ghost Soldiers': it was an apt description.

The rain had swollen the tributaries of the Brazos and it wasn't long before they came across the stream that King had crossed with his companions a few days before – but it was a stream no longer: to their eyes it was as big and fast flowing as any river.

'This is where we have to go,' said Lucas. 'We go to where the waters disappear into the rocks.'

Carter eyed the waters with some dismay. He had pictured some little body of water that they could cross in seconds, maybe getting their feet a little wet, but this already looked like a major obstacle.

'We go back a little way,' said Lucas, 'then we go down the left bank.' They did not demur at his suggestion, for it was one of those situations where if they did not press forwards the work would never be done, the men would return to camp and resist when the soldiers came to look for them, and would be at far greater risk of defeat holed up in their own territory.

They had little choice if they wanted to continue on their mission, so they followed him to the point where they thought they had the best chance of getting across. One by one the men got into the water, which reached above their knees. For the younger, smaller ones it went much higher, of course. They held their weapons up so that they at least kept them dry, and Carter walked with a pack on his back that had once been strapped to his horse. As he walked he looked back briefly to check, and saw that his men were still following him. The water was cold at that time of the morning and they were not warm anyway, so it was a shock to the system. Ghost soldiers on a ghost mission. For some reason he shuddered, in a way that was quite unrelated to the cold.

The river was not particularly wide, and soon they were across and out on to the opposite bank. Then the boy led them straight towards the crag into which the tributary flowed. Near the dark rock, it was almost complete darkness because the crag leaned over them like a threatening giant. Carter desperately longed for some light so that he could have a better look at where they were going, but he did not want to risk being detected by any sentries that had been posted by Valsquez on the rocks above, and they had all agreed that any kind of illumination was too risky.

Now the boy flitted ahead and took them towards the place that he could not see properly in the looming rock.

Carter squeezed into the gap behind their guide. It seemed to him impossible that this would lead to anywhere useful. Surely Lucas had gone to the wrong place? But as he pushed forwards he realized that the gap was opening up into a far more roomy interior – though 'roomy' was a relative term, because he could hear the water rushing beside him not too far away, and the banks of river were sloping steeply in here so it would be easy enough for a large man like him to fall back in – and since the water was far deeper here, it wasn't a pleasant thought.

They lit the torches they had brought with them. These were lengths of wood dipped in pitch. He lit one, and they stood there coughing slightly with the dark smoke it produced, but at least able now to see what was before them.

They were in a rough stone passage, and it was obvious from the workings that someone – in fact the work of many – had widened out a natural fissure in the rock beneath the fort.

Beside them the waters rushed downwards and into the rocks beyond. Lucas gestured upwards to the workings in the rock.

'See, *señor*, it curves up and comes out where we said. One man at a time can get up and one man at a time can go beyond and into the fort. We must talk little too, for the sound can echo.'

Carter could see that this was the most dangerous part of their mission for one reason alone. They had to get into the fort, and if the guards were alerted and arrived they would have very little time to deal with them. If only one or two were out and they failed to tackle the situation properly, most of them would be trapped in a bottleneck in the ground, and most of them would be trapped there until troops came in from the other side and killed them.

But it was a risk they would have to take.

The other men started coming in. They began to regroup, and Carter got the more slender, fitter ones to go first. This was their time.

Alice was determined that she was going to be part of the war against their enemies. She had just as much stake in this as Carter, one of the reasons being that he was hers from the moment they met, although neither had recognized the fact at the time.

One of the women whom she shared a tent with had been working on her crops when the village had been taken over, and she was dressed in a blue jacket and long linen trousers. The two women were about the same height, and Alice promised the woman a monetary reward when all this was over if she would agree to exchange their clothes. The woman was pleased with this, but seemed indifferent as to the reason for the exchange.

Alice was grateful for this, because when the dawn came and Carter came to the tent, she refused to open it, but wished him all the luck in the world. But then, as his men made their way out of the camp, she crawled out of the tent and followed them. It was a strategy that worked, because all the figures behind him were shadows, and he wasn't going to stop and count. The shock of entering the water was immense because she was so slim. She brought up the tail end of the men going into the cavern. They could hardly send her back when she appeared. Carter, it seemed, was waiting at the end. His torch sputtered out just before she went inside and he saw her face, and a curse of annoyance escaped from between his lips.

'Go back!' he said, 'I can't risk you.'

'No,' she said, 'no!' and pressed forwards. But at that precise second she lost her footing and fell into the rushing water.

It was much deeper than it had been upstream, and her slim body was carried forwards in a rush and towards the rocks beneath. She didn't even have a chance to scream because the coldness of the water cut away her breath.

Luckily, though, she got caught in some kind of rocky ledge – her legs came up against this and stopped her from being carried forwards. Then bizarrely, something dropped down from above – she heard it splash into the water in front of her. She reached out and found that her hands were dipping into a bucket, of all things. For a moment she held on to this as some kind of anchor against the water rushing past her, then it was torn from her grasp and pulled upwards.

She heard a noise and a torch was lighted behind

her. There was Carter: he had thrown off his pack and was wading into the water. He grabbed her jacket with a bear-like grasp and hauled her away from the opening into which she had nearly been dragged, and pulled her back on to the bank of the water, then hauled himself up. She could feel the anger coming off him like steam, but he did not reproach her for one reason alone: it was not the time and place for him to express this kind of emotion. He shouldered his burden and turned away and went up the rocky passage after his men with just two whispered words: 'Stay here!'

CHAPTER TWENTY

At the top of the twisting passage Quinto stood with Vetters. Lucas had already told them that when he had been up here before he had worked the grille loose that led to this particular passage. There was little noise because the sun was just beginning to rise. Every little noise seemed to them as if it was being heard by everyone in the fort, even though in reality they were small sounds. The two pushed at the rusty grate together – it was a couple of feet square. Slowly they lifted it and held it up in the air as they took it to one side of the opening.

The tension could be felt in the tunnel below them as the men waited to go forwards. It would take just one soldier to come along and raise the alarm, and they would be trapped like rats in a stony trap. They could have shots fired down on them or they could have bombs dropped on their heads. It was a terrifying prospect, and as the rusty grate made a scraping noise on the ground, opening an aperture above their heads, they waited for the noise that would herald their discovery ... but there was nothing.

They were helped by the fact that there was some noise coming from inside the barracks where King, had they but known this, had been deposited. There was a loud debate going on between King and the others, where he was sitting against a wall wrapped in blankets, eating scraps of meat and getting back some of his strength. He was urging them on, making them shout in anger.

Now it was time for the invaders to get up and into the fort. It turned out that they were behind one of the barracks, so fortuitously they were emerging in the one place where they were not going to be noticed, at least on that morning. Valsquez had been very careful to make sure that his men patrolled the entire fort, but this was the morning after they had been celebrating, and two guards could not keep their eyes on everything.

One by one the men emerged in the shadows behind the barracks, with Carter as the second last. It was an incredible feeling for them to be in the very place their compatriots had helped to rebuild, but it was the case.

With their weapons to hand they took up position behind each of the two barracks.

'Now,' said Carter, his voice barely above a whisper, but loud enough in the quiet of the morning.

Some of the young men ran forwards, guns in hand, while Vetters and Lucas went round to the door of the barracks in which the prisoners were being kept. The door was barred with a length of solid oak dropped into strong metal hooks, which was an effective method of securing the area without locks. Together Carter and Vetters lifted up the solid piece of wood and threw it to one side, with a clatter that shook the air.

The pair of them rushed inside and found their leader against the wall, some of the deadly chill taken off him by the blankets, his bodily warmth returned. Even in the dim light that filtered through the barred barrack windows they were shocked at the state of their leader, the torn clothing, the bruises on his face and neck, his bloodied forehead. But he stood up and threw off his blankets and looked Carter in the face with a stern, yet understanding expression.

'Give me guns,' he said. 'This is my fight too.'

In the meantime Sutton and his companions were confronting the armed guards, surprised to find only two of them. The guards reacted immediately to their peril by shouting incoherently in their own language while bringing up their weapons to fire on the invaders.

It was the first time that the invaders had fired in anger, and shots were exchanged. Fortunately for the new arrivals most of these went wide because the soldiers were busy scrambling towards the gates of the fort while turning to fire once or twice as they went, and yelling at the same time.

The rest of the soldiers came running. Many of

149

them were half dressed, and it was obvious that they were still the worse for wear from the night before. Even so, they were heavily armed because they always kept their weapons close to their sides even when they were sleeping off a drunken feast, and it was obvious that the invaders would have a good chance of being defeated. This was made plainer when Hernandez appeared in his full uniform. Strangely enough he didn't look as angry as he might – in fact he appeared delighted at the thought of going into battle. He had a sword at his side and he gave an almighty roar and withdrew this, then he pulled a pistol out of his belt and charged towards the invaders, firing as he went. One of the invaders, a man who wore a brown coat, rushed forward and took a shot at Hernandez with a Colt .45, but the shot went wide by a few inches. Hernandez, however, did not miss: his shot took the invader straight in the middle of the chest, and the young man's lifeblood spurted forth as he sprawled on the ground.

'Kill them, kill them all,' said Hernandez, roaring in his own tongue at the top of his voice and shooting at the invaders again. The new arrivals were armed, but they had not been properly trained due to lack of time. They had turned to fight the troops, and they were willing to do so, but it was clear that the soldiers were reacting in a trained manner and would soon defeat their enemy.

Quinto and his two companions were the only ones who appeared to have an understanding of what they were doing. They retreated in a strategic manner and fired on Hernandez' troops as they went.

The leader recognized at once that these were the ones to go for, as along with others they were withdrawing to continue battle alongside the barracks. Sword up, and screaming at the top of his voice 'Death to them all!', his pistol ready to fire, he followed after and his men streamed behind him, leaving behind some to cover those invaders who had already dropped their weapons in the face of the professional soldiers.

As Hernandez rounded the barracks he saw the people whom he had so lately routed, some ten in all backing off, but shooting at him, the bullets going wide. Killing the troops was not their only purpose. As the troops followed, with Hernandez at their head, the double doors at the side of the barracks opened and King came out with a gun in either hand, his eyes blazing with fury and the look in his eyes one of bitter anger.

Hernandez had only a split second to see this sight because King raised his guns and fired at point-blank range, blasting the commander back by several feet. Hernandez looked at the holes in his body with a sort of angry amazement.

'You. . . .' was all he said before falling on his back, a pool of blood spreading out beneath him.

But even as this happened the villagers who had been so cowed for so long came streaming out of the building where they had been imprisoned, men

and women alike. They ran at the remaining soldiers, and they did so in such numbers, and with
such overwhelming force, that the men barely had
time to retreat or even attack. Some shots were
fired, but the nature of the attack was such that only
one or two people were hit, and with minor wounds
at that, before they were able to overwhelm their
former captors.

Carter stepped out behind King. They had met
barely two minutes before, and when he saw what
was going on, King had gained a new strength from
the knowledge that his men had come to get him –
he had seized the weapons to hand and taken the
lead. He hadn't asked the rest of the captives to join
with him, but when they saw what he was doing they
had merely joined in.

There might have been a bloodbath there and
then, but King found it in him to roar out at the top
of his voice:

'No more killing! We are in the right, and that is
all.'

'It's true,' roared Carter in turn, 'we came to
rescue you, and we've done that.'

He and King marched towards the square and
found that the battle there was over, too. Ben, Alice,
Vetters and Sutter had held back, knowing from
facing these troops before that they would be quick
to respond. They had killed the two who had been
holding up the inexperienced fighters, and the rest,
numbering five in all, had surrendered.

Plenty of the soldiers had survived. They were

bundled back into the very barracks where they had imprisoned the villagers who had rebuilt the fort, and they were sealed in the same way.

Alice ran into the arms of Carter, who had a stern look on his face.

'You could have been killed,' he said.

'But I wasn't,' she answered quietly, and kissed him on the nose.

'Stop that,' he said, but not looking the least displeased.

But King wasn't finished.

'I have to see someone,' he said, stalking towards the headquarters, pushing his son away when the latter tried to go with him.

CHAPTER TWENTY-ONE

Jorge Valsquez was sitting in the padded chair that he had been using during their first confrontation. He was still wearing his blue and gold uniform, but his tri-corned hat lay on the ground. His dark hair was soaked in sweat, and his cheeks, instead of being blazing red as they were barely an hour before, had a dark tinge to them – and King, who knew the signs when he saw them, knew that he was looking at plague, that somehow, somewhere, Valsquez had picked up the germs from someone infected, and in his weakened state the sickness had raged through his body.

In other circumstances King would have shown mercy to someone who was obviously a sick man, but he was not going to do that for someone who had sown such misery. And Valsquez, sick though he was, was not about to give up without a fight. He pulled out his dagger and lunged at the new arrival.

King could have shot him in the head right away, but he had a point to make. He pulled to one side and grabbed the wrist of the revolutionary and compressed it with all his strength so that the man had to drop the weapon.

'Kill me now,' said Valsquez.

'No,' said King, and bodily drew the man outside. King was also in a state of near collapse, but this was an act that had to be carried out.

'No,' said Alice once they were outside, looking at the man who was being forced to move in front of King. 'I see it in him, the signs of the disease.'

'The water,' said Carter, 'he must have drank the water, remember – that well over there, it must tap into the underground river.'

'Then I have killed him,' she said, her face ashen now that she was faced with the results of being a carrier of infection.

Valsquez ignored her and looked straight ahead, seemingly ignoring the gun at his head, too. Those who had been his prisoners were already shrieking and calling now that they had caught sight of him.

'String him up!'

'Riddle him with bullets!'

'Carter,' King looked grimly at his old friend. 'I think you brought something of mine with you.'

'I guess I did,' said Carter. He handed the bag to his friend.

'Keep an eye on this one,' said King. He walked forwards across the square, people clearing out of the way for him. 'Get out of here,' he said, 'all of you. Assemble down by the barracks.'

He took out the barrel of gunpowder and fitted it into a niche near the bottom of the west wall. He took a handful of the gunpowder and trickled it expertly in a line away from the keg and towards those standing there. Valsquez squirmed and looked near to collapse as he stood there, but such was his willpower that he remained upright.

'You fool!' he said in a hoarse voice. 'You destructive fool!'

'You killed my youngest child and my wife,' said King. He took out a match and struck it on the rough cobbles. There was a moment when nothing happened, and then the flame licked along the ground as King and his companions pulled away. King snatched at the arms of the dictator, but Valsquez gave an almost inhuman scream and tore away from the grasp of his captor. King was not about to chase after him – indeed he made sure that they had all ducked safely inside the building. He was armed now, and once they were inside he looked out, the Colt in his hand as he aimed at the would-be dictator.

Valsquez was too late for what he was trying to do: the flame reached the gunpowder before he did, and there was a roar that sounded as if it came from the throat of a giant lion, then the courtyard rumbled and shook from what seemed like a minor earthquake – and miraculously Valsquez was flung backwards by the blast and survived. He got to his feet and stared up at the wall, and he laughed loud and long.

Despite the black smoking crater in the ground the wall seemed to be fairly intact. Tattered, ragged and ill, Valquez turned and held out his arms, a sneer on his features as he turned and gazed at those he had used.

'My greatest triumph: when they hear of this they will come – my people will come and the north will be defeated, and they shall have what is theirs.'

His words had not been loud, barely whispered, but they had carried in them the power that the man must once have had that had inspired so many people to join him in his quest for power.

King raised his gun again, knowing that any shot he fired would kill the dictator – but it would also make the bandit a folk hero, a carrier of myth, who might prove to be a better rallying point when dead than alive, a martyr at the hands of the brutal usurpers who had taken his land.

The wall, though, had other ideas, for there was a sound that Valsquez had heard much of lately, the sound of stone breaking apart – and as he stood there a groan came from the very foundations of the fort itself, stone rumbled on stone like thunder, and the wall came crashing down upon him. It happened in seconds, it took so little time – and Valsquez vanished from sight beneath the stones of the monument he had created through enslavement.

King stood in the graveyard in Purgatory, holding his hat before him in both hands. There was a stone now on the grave, the words on it carved with his own two hands: 'To Marie my wife, and Ranald my son. You live forever in my heart.' And below this was the date of their deaths. Beside him was his oldest son and they waited there for what seemed like a long time, the early snows of winter falling from above unheeded as they paid their respects to those they were going to leave behind, but who would never really leave them.

Neither of them needed to say anything, and at last they put on their hats, turned away, and walked out of the wooden gateway with the crossbar above that bore the word 'Cemetery'.

They went to the ruins of their old home, and without a word the boy and his father dug into the ground and took out a buried metal box, the key of which jangled on King's key ring. He stowed the metal container in his saddlebag, then swung up on to the back of the grey mare.

'If only we'd left here and gone to the city a year earlier,' said King. 'I knew we were getting to the last of the precious metals, but they paid me so well to patch 'em up, this box is full of gold dust.' He stopped, and his voice was gruff when he spoke again. 'Son, let's get out of here, we'll build a new life in the city. I can be a real doctor now' – but they both knew as they rode away that there were some wounds that would never heal.

They went out of town and were met by Carter, Vetters and Sutton on their own horses. Two others waited nearby – Lucas and Alice.

'Guess this is it,' said Carter.

'I thought you were going to retire to the city, Jos,' said his old friend, without smiling but with a lighter tone to his voice.

'Guess that one's out of the window,' said Carter with a faint nod towards the waiting woman. Alice smiled at them, and they could tell why he was staying. 'Lucas is staying on too, and I guess we've got a ranch to rebuild.'

'I don't want to go back to Valensis,' said Lucas in a low voice. He did not need to add the phrase 'too many memories'.

'Well,' said the man who liberated him, 'I guess the fact your cousins have elected to stay on will help give the place a jolt.'

'There is much building to do,' said Lucas, 'but the fort will never be used again.' This was true, because after they had been liberated, the Texas Rangers had arrived, led by Helmuth, who had escaped at the same time as Ben. The old fort had been brought to the ground by dynamite, so those villagers who remained had plenty of building materials for their work.

'Well, gents, it's been a pleasure knowing you,' said Carter, doffing his hat to them all. 'But I never was one for long goodbyes. So take care all you here, and once you get established in the town come back and there'll be a mighty big welcome waiting for you all.'

'And that goes for me, too,' said Alice. They all turned and rode off, and the remaining four watched them go.

It was a beautiful day, still early in the morning. King turned and looked at his companions.

'Guess it's time to make our way in the world and forget all types of purgatory.' They said nothing, but as they rode on and the long journey continued they began to joke and laugh and talk about all kinds of nonsense just to pass the time before they started their lives anew in the big city.